ERAS OF US

SHANNON O'CONNOR

Copyright © 2024 Shannon O'Connor
All rights reserved.

All rights reserved. No part of this publication may be reproduced, distributed, or transmitted in any form or by any means, except in the case of brief quotations embodied in critical reviews and articles.

No use of AI was used to create this book, cover or edit any of the following. Please do NOT use my words, cover, or anything from this book in an AI form to feed AI.

Any resemblance to persons alive or dead is purely coincidental.

Cover by *Cruel Ink Editing & Design*.

Edited & Proofread by Victoria Ellis of *Cruel Ink Editing & Design*.

Formatted by Shannon O'Connor.

❀ Created with Vellum

Content Warnings

Please note some of these might be considered spoilers for parts of the story.

- Grief/Loss of parent
(on page)
- Alcoholism
(On page- not main characters)
- Emotional abuse
(On page- not between main characters)

ERAS OF US

PLAYLIST

Never Really Over - Katy Perry

I Like Me Better - Lauv

Different - Joshua Bassett

Your Type - Carly Rae Jepsen

The Golden Years - Joshua Bassett

Please Please Please - Sabrina Carpenter

Dancing With Tears In My Eyes - Joshua Bassett

tell me it's okay - gnash

So Close - NOTD, Felix Jaehn, Captain Cuts, Georgia Ku

Girl Of Your Dreams - Dylan

What If I Love You - Gatlin

You Won't Forget About Me, Right? - NERIAH

Stupid - Cate

ghosts! - Sophie Cates

ERAS OF US

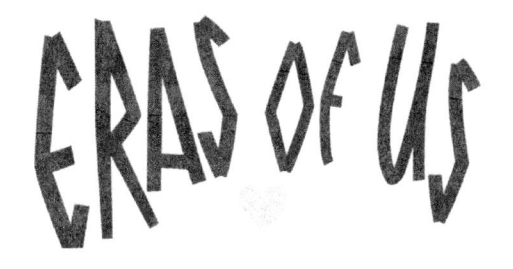

1. You ruined New York City for me
2. Another Life
3. Eras of Us
4. Sex (with my ex)
5. Joyride
6. Pretending
7. Guess We Lied...
8. The One
9. Feel
10. Her Body is Bible
11. Girls Girls Girls
12. Shh...Don't Say it
13. Strangers
14. Lead Me On
15. Over My Head
16. Lover
17. Antidote
18. Crush
19. She Said
20. Butterflies
21. Serial Heartbreaker
22. Avalanche
23. Silence
24. Attached to You
25. Healing
26. Birthday Girl
27. Butterflies
28. Wasted Youth

To FLETCHER

"These are the eras of us, a story of love"
  - FLETCHER

1. You ruined New York City for me

RIVER

"Holy shit, your tits look phenomenal in that top." I gasp as Cari emerges from the bathroom. Her boobs are on full display in a lace bodysuit that she's paired with black denim shorts.

"I know, right?" Cari smirks and curls her red lips at me.

"Is your tattoo healed?" I ask nervously. I don't see the end results of my client's tattoos after the healing process—well, not typically, anyway. They come to me, but I'm rarely tagged in fully healed photos. People seem way more excited to post fresh tattoo photos than photos weeks later. My best friend is one of the only exceptions, but I always worry about her aftercare.

"Yes, see?" She shows me her left shoulder where her version of the goddess Aphrodite is on display. Damn, my work came out great, if I may say so myself. I run my hands over her skin, and she's right; it's fully healed.

"You're the only client whose tattoos I get to see in every stage."

"Client?" Cari gasps and clutches her chest.

"Oh shush, you know what I mean." I roll my eyes.

"I'm just a client to you?" she teases and cracks a smile. That's my best friend, the overdramatic one of us.

1

"You're obviously more than that." I pick up my lip gloss and run it across my lips as I frown at my hair.

My curls are wild and unruly today. I mean, honestly, they're unruly most days. But for the concert tonight, I actually want them to look a little more tame. I think about it but decide there's not much I can do at this point. I slide on my round sunglasses and decide to take a selfie. My outfit is cute as hell, and tonight needs to be documented.

I'm in my usual all-black attire, but tonight I'm donning a tube top and miniskirt combo that makes my legs look a million miles long. I slide on my usual Doc Martens and toss on a dark-wash jean jacket and snap a few photos.

"I thought I was the social media influencer; since when does River take selfies?" Cari raises an eye in suspicion.

"I don't know. I wanted to document tonight." I shrug.

"Well, at least let your *client* get in a few," she teases again and steps next to me in the full-length mirror.

I have to admit, we both look hot. I mean, with all of Cari's tattoos, which were courtesy of having a best friend for a tattoo artist, and my outfit, I'm impressed. We clean up nicely. This is much better than our usual sweatpants and oversized T-shirt combo.

"Got your wallet?" Cari asks as she slips hers into her clear plastic mini backpack. I hate that concert venues only allow clear bags, so I slip all the things I might need into my front pockets. My phone has digital copies of all my cards, so I don't need much.

"Yup, all packed." I smile.

"We should get going then. I don't want to be standing outside sweating my ass off in line."

"Wouldn't want that."

After flipping off my bedroom lights, we head out of my apartment and toward the subway. It's hotter than I expect outside for a mid-May night.

I'm sweating by the time we make it to the depths of the subway, so I slip off my jacket. It doesn't help that my hair is making me a thousand times hotter.

I slide my metro card through the turnstile and follow Cari to the Q train. It's not too crowded for this time of day, and we manage to get a seat in an air conditioned car. Cari doesn't seem as sweaty as me. Her hair is only to her shoulders, and it's thinner than mine, so she doesn't have the same problem as me.

I look around the subway as we head underground. My phone loses service, so I distract myself by reading a few of the ads on the ceiling above me. There's one for Tinder, one for some food app—but it's the last one that makes me pause. It's an ad for a movie that came out almost a decade ago. It makes no sense, considering all the other ads on this train are current. I shake my head, trying to rid myself of thoughts of the old movie. I'm all too familiar with it. At one point, it used to play constantly when I was at my ex's house. It's her favorite movie, and for a little while, it had become mine, too.

Swallowing feels harder than normal. I haven't given much thought to Aspen in a while now. I've come a long way, because when our breakup was still fresh, I had a really difficult time. We broke up four or five years ago; I've lost track. Now, it's rare to have even a fleeting thought about her.

Right now, though…well, right now, the thought of her and this movie is making me freeze. It's silly, really. It isn't like I still care about her. I don't even know what she's up to. I blocked her on all of my socials a long time ago.

So why is thinking about her right now so difficult?

"Come on!" Cari grabs my hand, and we run off the train at the last second before the doors close. I must've been in my own little world, because I didn't even feel the train stop.

"It says it's a fifteen minute walk, but it's not like we're paying an Uber to go a few blocks during rush hour," Cari explains, looking at her phone.

"Walking is okay." I nod and shake out the thoughts of Aspen. It doesn't matter. She's my past, and last I heard, she's out in California anyway.

Cari leads the way, and I'm grateful I have a few moments to collect my thoughts. Seeing that ad was jarring, and I need to get back in the right headspace. The streets are busy, so I'm weaving in and out of people that are clearly tourists. Don't people know how to stay on their side of the street? Surely that's the rule in every other state in this country, no? It'll only get worse in the summertime with the influx of tourists wanting to visit.

"Are you okay?" Cari looks at me with one eyebrow raised.

"Yes, just hoping there won't be a big line."

"Probably not; we're early." Cari smiles and we turn the block to see the venue. Madison Square Garden is a large venue with thousands of seats. We're on the floor, which means we don't *technically* have seats. I'd take the pit over being far away from the stage any day.

There're about ten other people waiting outside the venue. From my quick observation, the crowd seems to be mostly women and a few gay men. They are all sporting some sort of Pride gear, whether it's a keychain or a more obvious flag worn as a cape. It makes sense. LULY, although relatively new to the scene, is an out and proud lesbian. She recently came out, and that only seemed to make her more popular than before. She stuck to smaller venues typically, until very recently.

Cari and I get in line, and when the doors open at six, we're the first ones into the place. We head straight for the bar. She hit her weed pen on the way to the venue, but I'm not much for that stuff. It's legal now, but anytime I've tried it, it's just made me all nervous and anxious. Cari orders her usual—a vodka cranberry—while I get a tequila sunrise.

Cari and I make our way toward the stage. We end up standing on the left side, and there's even a banister for us to lean on if our legs get tired.

"Which song are you most excited for?" Cari asks as she uses her phone camera to check her lipstick.

"I'm not sure, maybe 'Mine' or 'Don't fuck your ex'," I say. LULY has range, and honestly, anything on her setlist is sure to bang.

"Yes! 'Don't fuck your ex' is such a fucking banger. I play it every time I'm in the shower." Cari squeals.

"Even though you're still fucking Olivia?" I raise an eyebrow.

"Excuse me! I haven't done that in forever." She waves me off.

"Two weeks ago, is not forever," I point out.

"Oh, you with your good memory." She rolls her eyes.

"I'm so sorry to interrupt, but are you Cari? Like, Cari Moore?" Two teenage looking girls ask, interrupting us.

"I am." Cari smiles.

"Oh, my gosh! I told you so!" One of the girls practically squeals in excitement as she looks at her friend.

"Could we get a photo with you?" one of the girls asks.

"Of course." Cari smiles and I offer to take the photo. I'm used to this kind of thing happening more and more lately. Cari has a big following, but she's been getting even more brand deals lately, and she's just gaining even more of an audience. Thankfully, it isn't going to her head, so she's still just *Cari* to me.

"Thank you so much!" The girls giggle.

"Of course. Just remember, no filters." Cari winks. She's built her entire brand on the premise of natural beauty, so she always asks fans not to filter the photos they take with her. It's pissed off a few of the brand reps she's partnered with, but that's her way of having the trash take itself out.

The girls smile, running away. "You just made their week," I tell her.

"Eh, it's just nice to meet people who follow me." Cari shrugs like it's no big deal.

"I'm glad I don't have to worry about you getting a big head from all this fame," I tease.

"Never. I'm still me. Just with half a million more followers."

I sip my drink and watch as the road crew sets up the band's equipment. We're seeing an all-female band, and thanks to my Instagram stalking, I've found out they are mostly queer, too. I'm not delusional—I know I don't have a chance of going home with someone from the band. I'm not a groupie, after all, but hey, it's nice to daydream. It's been a while since I've hooked up with anyone; I highly doubt I'll end my dry spell with a famous musician.

I haven't been on an intentional hiatus, but I'm getting older. I sewed my wild oats in my early twenties after my breakup with Aspen. The ending of a five-year relationship will do that to a woman, I guess. Now, I'm almost thirty, and the only thing on my mind is settling down with someone to join me in my sweats on long nights. Tonight, the idea of hooking up with someone just for the fun of it seems like fun, though. It's been almost seven months.

"Who are you looking at with sex eyes?" Cari asks, trying to see who I'm staring at.

"With what?!" I nearly choke on my drink.

"Sex eyes. Your eyes got all dark and lust-filled. Was it the drummer? She's cute as fuck." Cari smiles, clearly approving.

"Yeah, I don't know. I was just thinking it's been a while since I had sex. I could afford a night of fun." I shrug.

"Yes, you could. Maybe we can sneak backstage after the show." Cari wiggles her eyebrows. We've never used her social status to get backstage anywhere before, but I'm sure we probably could. I smile at the drummer, and she smiles back. I sip my drink, hoping to conceal my blush. Maybe we could go backstage or something.

It isn't the worst idea in the world…

2. Another Life

ASPEN

"You don't mind doing our makeup, too?" Liz asks as she takes a seat on Max's bed.

"Nah, we should have enough time before the concert. What are you guys up to tonight?" I ask Liz.

"Rachel and I are headed out on a blind—double—date. If it sucks, we're going to a new club downtown." Liz flips through a magazine Max left behind.

"Fun." I smile. Things have been a little awkward between Liz and I lately. We were hooking up for several months, but I ended it somewhat abruptly last month. Well, it had been on my mind for a while, but I'm sure for her it felt abrupt. Since then, I've been sort of avoiding being alone with her. Unfortunately for me, I'm currently making small talk since Max is still in the shower.

"Yeah, it's these two Wall Street women. Rachel is more into it than I am, but whatever." Liz shrugs.

"You HAVE to tell me what to wear!" Rachel storms into the room in her underwear holding three different hangers full of clothes. It isn't unlike her, honestly—these theatrics. She has no boundaries, and this isn't the first time I've seen her like this. Max's roommates are used to me, considering I spend most of my free time here.

"What are the options?" Liz asks, setting down the magazine.

"Well, I was going for classy but what if we end up at the club after? I don't want to look like someone's *mom*."

"What about that dress? But with the blazer." I point to a pretty dress as I attempt to combine two outfits for her. Rachel pauses and then smiles.

"Yes! You're a life saver." She stands on her toes to press her lips to my cheek, and I blush. It's not lost on me that Liz scowls into her phone.

Rachel disappears just as Max reappears; she has dripping-wet hair and a thick black towel wrapped around her body. Liz rolls her eyes, and Max drops her towel as she stands in front of her closet to grab her clothes. I turn away, because although seeing my best friend naked does nothing for me, I also don't need to stare. Max is hot—if you're into butch women with masculine features. But honestly, that's not really my type. I'm a femme who often gravitates to other femmes. Like Liz, for instance. She's as girly and feminine as they come, down to her pretty, pink-painted nails.

"The concert starts at seven, so we need to be there around six forty-five. My friend put our name down, so we don't have to wait in any lines," Max says, and I turn to watch as they cuff the shoulders of their black T-shirt. Their all-black attire is a staple for them, all the way down to the black boots and the cuffed black jeans.

"Okay. I'm doing Liz and Rachel's makeup first. Then I'll do mine, and we'll be good to go," I explain.

"Nice, we have time so no worries." Max takes a seat at their desk and flicks on their desktop.

"Are those the photos you took for the magazine?" I ask, looking at the photos she's currently flipping through.

"Yeah, I have to pick my favorites and edit them before they get approved." Max furrows their eyebrows.

"Can you do my makeup like this?" Liz pulls up a photo on her phone. It's a photo of some celebrity I don't know, but the makeup is easy enough. It's a little darker than I would've done for her skin tone, but she's the client.

"Yeah, let me grab my bag." I head to the living room and get my supplies from the coffee table. I stop to pet Frisky, Max and her roommates' dog. He's just sleeping under the coffee table like normal.

"Are you dressed?" I ask Liz. She doesn't look ready, but one can never tell with her.

"*No*, you think I'm wearing this out?" She scoffs and heads to her bedroom. She's wearing a T-shirt and jean shorts, so it could've been what she planned on wearing, but apparently not.

"She's still pissed you guys aren't sleeping together. She'll cool down eventually," Max says quietly, not looking away from her computer.

"Isn't it better I ended things before anyone caught feelings?" I sigh. I thought I was doing the right thing.

"Well, it might be too late for that." Max turns and her mouth forms a line. Of course, I should've realized the signs, but I'm oblivious when it comes to that kind of thing apparently.

"Now, I'm ready." Liz comes back, and this time she's wearing a little black dress. She's clearly waiting for some kind of a reaction from me, but I don't give her one. I need to help her get over me.

"Cool, take a seat and I'll get started." Liz huffs but takes a seat on the edge of the bed. I pull a chair over and sit in front of her. She closes her eyes, and I get to work.

Liz is beautiful, and I didn't suddenly stop liking her. I enjoyed it a lot, honestly. But, I knew it wasn't going anywhere. I had been sleeping with her for almost a year, and I felt nothing but friendship toward her. I wonder if I'll ever feel something toward another person again, to be honest. Maybe I'm stuck in this unfeeling limbo that I seem to have trapped myself in. But that's another box of worms I don't want to open right now.

"Rachel, pull up a photo of what you want so I know what you're looking for!" I call. She pokes her head into Max's room and purses her lips.

"Can you do my makeup like you did for Grant's wedding?" She cocks her head.

"Yeah." I nod. That's easy and a lot less than what Liz wants.

Liz is only half done because we have a lot of layers for the dark eye makeup. I tuck her dark red hair behind her ear and continue applying her blush. I know my life would be simple if I just stayed with Liz. I mean, we could probably be happy, get married, and move in together. The whole nine yards, but then why does the thought of that make me feel like I'm suffocating?

"Almost done?" Liz asks, peeking open one eye.

"Yeah, give me two minutes." She closes her eyes, and I put the final touches on.

Liz looks in Max's full-length mirror on the back of her door. She smiles and turns to me. "Thanks."

"No worries." I smile.

Liz disappears and Rachel floats into the room a minute later. She takes Liz's place on the bed while I grab fresh brushes for her. She's wearing the outfit we picked out for her, and it looks even cuter on. She's clearly excited for tonight; her leg won't stop bouncing. I'm used to nervous clients, mostly working with jittery brides—it's a hazard of the job.

"I hate blind dates. A friend of mine from work set us up. I'm worried it's a case of a straight person attempting to hookup his only gay friends," Rachel explains.

"Those are the worst," Max chimes in.

"Well, maybe it'll work out. If not, at least you have a good backup plan."

"My backup plan is the club with Liz and then an early night with my vibrator." Rachel laughs.

"I heard that!" Liz calls.

"Good, then you won't bother me later." Rachel shrugs.

"Just remember that we share a wall." Max stares at Rachel.

"Oh, yeah, like you can say anything. Every time you bring a girl home it's like an at-home porno."

"It's not my fault that the women I bring home enjoy themselves. Oh wait, yes it is." Max chuckles.

"We get it, you pull a lot of pussy." I roll my eyes. "Well, hopefully your dates are good." I smile as I put the finishing touches on Rachel.

"Thanks, babe." Rachel blows me a kiss and disappears.

"Can I borrow some eyeliner?" Max asks.

"Yup," I hand her the darkest one I have with me. Max adds some under her eyes and hands it back to me.

I quickly change into the fishnets, jean skirt, and cropped concert T-shirt. I slide on my combat boots and then apply some quick makeup. It's more than I usually wear, but I know Max is bringing her camera today, and I assume there will be some photos. Rather than looking bare-faced on Instagram, I opted for a concert look.

"Ready? I can call an Uber," Max says, looking at her phone.

"Yup." I nod.

The concert is in midtown, and Max lives in Bushwick, so there's no way we're attempting to grab a train during rush hour. An Uber is much more reliable at this time of day—especially coming from Brooklyn. Max calls one and we pull up to the venue just in time. We sidestep the line and head inside. Max grabs a drink at the bar, so I hold her camera while she waits. I know how big of a deal that is, so I hold on tight until she's back.

"Let's go." Max nods her head toward the stairs, and we're let behind a rope to the balcony. There's a table reserved for us by the front of the stage. Max isn't on a job, but she'll probably end up selling some of the photos she takes tonight. She can't help it; she just loves her job.

LULY starts the concert exactly on time, which is almost unheard of, but I'm not complaining. Damn, she's even hotter in person. Her blonde hair is flowing all around her, dressed in a barely-there bra and a pair of colorful leggings. She's hot *and* into women. She sings her hit songs first, and the crowd goes wild. Everyone is belting the lyrics with her, including me; it's a banger for a reason.

"This one is new, but I hope you'll like it," she announces right before the drummer starts. It's slower than her usual beat, but somehow I'd still classify it as pop. It's the lyrics that get me, though.

It's all about letting someone go because the timing was off but still loving them.

My heart lurches as I think about River. It's been a while since she crossed my mind, but it isn't the first time I've thought of her. She pops into my head randomly, like a catchy tune I just can't seem to shake. I guess some part of me will always love her. That's just how it is with first loves, right?

I look around at the crowd, mainly people's heads. There's one person who catches my eye—which is unreal because there are *so* many people here. A head of crazy, untamed, dark-brown curls is dancing to the song.

River?

My heart stops. There's no way. Of all the places to see her, she's here tonight? I squint to see, but the person turns the other way and all I can see is her hair. It's probably just a coincidence. I was thinking about River and then I see her in the crowd. It doesn't mean anything, except maybe I'm going a little bit crazy. I haven't seen her in years. What are the chances?

I focus my attention back on LULY and sing along to the rest of the concert. Even though there's something tugging on my heart to make me look at the woman with the messy curls—something urging me to go down and see if that really was River after all. I ignore it, River and I are in the past. Years in the past. Even if she's here, there's no reason I should care.

Still, despite knowing I shouldn't…

I do.

3. Eras of Us

RIVER

"**H**oly shit! SHE'S SO TALENTED!" Cari yells over the crowd.

"SHE IS!" I yell back.

LULY just finished her set, so the roadies are cleaning up, but there's still random music playing. The crowd is slow to move through the venue, but that's how it always is. I'm in no rush to be stuck in a group of people not moving.

"I HAVE TO PEE!" I yell to Cari, and she nods, holding up her phone. I give her a quick thumbs-up, knowing what she means. She needs to take a few quick shots for Instagram.

I make my way toward the bathroom, but it's just as crowded. It's like everyone in the venue had the same idea: run to the bathroom. I'm tempted to go in the men's room, but there's a burly-looking security guard standing outside it, and I know my chances of getting in are low. I make my way back toward Cari; I don't have to pee badly enough to stand in a long line. Surely, I can hold it until we get back to my apartment.

I spot Cari by the stage; she's probably *live* on Instagram, because she's holding her phone up and talking while panning around the space. I see her lips moving and then notice a masculine-looking woman taking pictures near her. I get closer and realize she's taking photos of Cari. I'm about to go ask if the person wants me to introduce them to Cari when I stop in my tracks.

Right next to the masculine woman with the camera, is none other than Aspen Wheeler. The former love of my life. I can feel my heart actually skip a beat, and then it goes a hundred beats per second. Do I say something? Do I turn around? After our breakup, Aspen disappeared to California, and I never worried about having to see her. So her presence *here*, in *New York*, is completely jarring. I wish my fight-or-flight would kick in because I'm standing less than twenty feet from her, and at any second, she could look this way. I'll have no choice but to say something if we make eye contact. Maybe that's what I want. I could stand still, and she'd have to make the choice of what to do next.

Before I can overthink it some more, Cari calls my name. Loud as day, she yells, "RIVER! COME HERE!" She waves me over, completely oblivious to my mental freakout. I start to walk toward her as Aspen's neck snaps around and she locks eyes with me. I walk right past her, and I can feel her eyes on me as I reach Cari.

"I thought you didn't see me. I just went *live*, and I got all the shots I need. Did you pee?" Cari asks and I gulp. My mouth feels completely dry—like that time I got cotton mouth from smoking Cari's weed in high school.

"Um, no there was a line," I manage.

"River?" Aspen's voice rings familiarly in my ears. I let out a quick breath and turn to face my ex…the woman who turned my life upside down.

"Aspen." It comes out quieter than I expect.

"Aspen?" Cari's voice twists, and I can tell she's thinking about punching Aspen in the face, but there are too many witnesses.

"W-what are you doing here?" Aspen asks.

"Me? What are *you* doing here?" I ask, even more surprised. *Why isn't she far away in California?*

"I, uh, moved back about six months ago." She brushes her dark-blonde hair behind her ear.

"Riv, we can go…" Cari nudges me.

"I'm okay, why don't you give us a minute?" I look at her and then back at Aspen. It feels like everything is shaking. Seeing her here after so long—my world is suddenly standing still.

"Okay." Cari gives me a look like she isn't sure this is the best idea, but she walks away.

"How are you?" Aspen smiles and I can tell she isn't just asking; she really wants to know.

"I'm good. How are you?" I smile back.

"I'm good, actually. It's just weird being back in New York. I don't know how, but I forgot the winters are this cold." She laughs. *Fuck*. How long has it been since I heard her laugh? Had it always made my stomach do flips like this?

"You never were a fan of the winter," I say, remembering so many winter nights spent inside. Not that it's my favorite, but Aspen didn't even like *looking* at snow let alone being outside in it.

"I thought I saw you tonight. I recognized your curls in the crowd." Aspen reaches out as if she's going to touch one, but she pulls back at the last second.

"You did?" I ask, surprised.

"I did. I guess I shouldn't have been surprised to see you here with Cari; I'm glad you have her." She smiles.

"Going on twenty years of friendship," I say proudly.

"I almost didn't recognize her with blonde hair." She points to her hair.

"She went to back to natural when she became an influencer," I explain.

"Ah." Aspen nods.

"Well, we should get going," I say quietly. I don't' know how to end whatever this reunion is, but this seems like the best way.

"Sure." Aspen shrugs but neither of us walk away. Where do we go from here? Do we shake hands? Hug? What's the protocol for something like this?

"Would it be weird if we hugged?" Aspen asks.

"Yes." We both laugh. "But you can hug me." I smile.

Aspen steps forward with her arms extended and pulls me in for a tight hug. All the nerves in my body disappear as our bodies touch. Not in a sexual way, but in an intimate way. I relax, her familiar scent fills my nose. Her hair smells like that shampoo I could never remember the name of. I always just associated it with peaches. I close my eyes and remember how just a hug from her made my entire day better. Aspen's arms are wrapped around my waist, and I have mine over her shoulders. I slump into her; I haven't felt like this in years. It's almost like everything and everyone around us has disappeared, and now it's just us. Like I'm home again. It's all consuming—and terrifying.

We're hugging longer than socially acceptable, and I'm aware of it. Longer than exes hug, for sure. But I don't want to let her go yet. I'm afraid when I let her go, I will actually have to *let her go* again. Eventually, we both begin to pull away, and I clear my throat. It's fine. We're fine.

"I guess I'll see you around?" Aspen says but it comes out like a question.

"Your friend seems to be getting along quite well with Cari." I motion toward where her masculine friend is clearly flirting with Cari. She's tucked Cari's hair behind her ear and has her hand on her arm. Cari's laughing is in full force. It's a tell-tale sign she's flirting back.

"Shit, honestly she'd be good for Max. Maybe she'd keep Max on her toes," Aspen muses. I didn't mean to avoid her question, but I'm surprised how well they're hitting it off.

"I don't want to interrupt what could be the start of something," I say, and it's half true.

"I guess we should keep talking then." Aspen grins. "Did you end up finishing art school?"

"I did, but I don't really use my degree. Not in the typical way, anyway. I'm a tattoo artist," I say proudly.

"Shit, that's so cool!" Aspen gushes. "Wait! Is that your work on Cari? She's like, covered in tats."

"Yeah, perks of being the best friend. She let me use her skin when I was learning so I've been covering up old practice ones lately," I explain.

"That's amazing. I still have the one you gave me in the basement with that tattoo gun you bought online. Remember when your mom found us and thought I was going to get a disease?" Aspen laughs as we both recall the memory. My mother was a bit high-strung, and walking in on me tattooing my girlfriend in her basement was enough to almost give her a stroke.

"You still have it?" I'm shocked. No way should that still be in her system; I doubt the ink was even FDA approved or safe.

Aspen pulls up her sleeve and shows me the small heart that's on the bicep of her arm. It's faded but it's still there. I reach out and touch it. It doesn't feel like anything, but a shock of electricity jolts me when I touch her skin. I pull my fingers back instantly and then look at her. Did she feel that, too?

"Do you have a shop in the city?"

"Yeah, it's uh, an all-female and queer-owned shop in the village," I tell her.

"Well, when I'm due for more ink I know where to go. I had this sleeve done in California, but it isn't anything special." She shrugs, motioning to the full sleeve she's sporting on the other arm. It's mainly floral elements; it's cool, but nothing striking.

"Are you working?" I ask, not sure how to bring it up. She wasn't in college when we were together, but she did have dreams we used to talk about.

"Yeah, I'm a professional makeup artist. Mainly weddings but some movies and things. It's a cool gig." She smiles. *Makeup artist*, that suits her.

"How do you know your friend?" I ask.

"Max? We connected on Instagram. She's a photographer, and I worked with her a bit when she was in Cali. When I moved back, I connected with her. Lived with her for a little, too."

"Ah, you're not living with her anymore?" I don't know why I'm even asking. She hasn't mentioned a new girlfriend. That's something she'd mention, right?

"No, I had to move back in with my mom." She tenses up at the mention of her mother.

"How's your mom doing?"

"Fine." She doesn't elaborate, like I expect her to. I'm sure there's a story there, but it's not my place to ask.

"I didn't expect to run into you tonight," I blurt out.

"Same. Kind of threw me for a loop." She relaxes at the change of subject.

We both pause. What the hell do you say to an ex that you haven't seen in almost five years? We've gone through the small talk and catching up, but I don't want the conversation to end yet. I don't want her to leave. The thought of her walking away and us saying goodbye all over again makes my heart ache. We both smile at each other, clearly unsure of what to say. This isn't the night either of us had planned. I mean, a few hours ago, I was fantasizing about going home with the drummer, not running into my ex.

Wait! Maybe that's it.

Maybe Aspen and I were supposed to run into each other for a little one-night thing. She went to California right after our breakup, so we never had the chance for post-breakup sex. Maybe we could have one night of fun with someone familiar and put our past behind us once and for all. It's silly, but the way she's looking at me right now tells me I'm not alone in this thinking. I glance at Cari and Max, but they're too busy flirting to even pay us any attention.

"Are you busy tonight?" I ask, being bold and making the first move.

"Like now?"

"Yeah." I nod.

"Nah, I was going to hang out with Max, but it seems like she's hitting it off with Cari. Why?" Aspen raises an eyebrow.

"Wanna come over?" I ask like it's no big deal what she says either way.

I ask like the thought of her saying *no* wouldn't completely crush me.

"Uh, yeah. I think I do." Aspen smiles back, and I remind myself that tonight is just sex with my ex.

Nothing more.

4. Sex (with my ex)

ASPEN

When River asks me to come over, I almost forget how to breathe. Thankfully, I recover quickly and I'm able to formulate a proper response. It's the last thing I had expected to come out of River's mouth, honestly. But then again, I also didn't expect her to be so kind to me—considering the way I had left. It seems like River is willing to put all of that behind us now. It almost feels too good to be true.

She stands next to Cari, clearly in a heated discussion about what this might mean, while Max looks at me expectantly.

"That's River," I explain. Her name is explanation enough; Max knows the story.

"Oh, shit." Max's eyes go wide, and she covers her mouth.

"She just asked me to come over."

"Damn, like to hookup?" She looks impressed. I don't blame her, River is a catch. Five foot eight and exudes pure sex appeal with goddess-like hair and a face to match.

"I think so? She kinda gave me a look, but honestly, who knows."

"Her friend is cool," Max says nonchalantly. That's her way of saying she's super into Cari.

"She's single. You should go for it." It wouldn't be the worst thing in the world to have our best friends together—at least for tonight.

"Hmm, I just might." Max glances over at them. Cari and River seemed to have cleared up whatever was going on, and they're hugging now.

"Ready?" River asks with a smile, walking back over.

"Yup." I nod. I'm not about to let this opportunity slip through my fingers. I've dreamed about being with River again, even if it's only for one night.

Max slides her arm around Cari's waist, and they head out the side door. I follow River toward the main exit, and she pulls up the Uber app on her phone. Two minutes later, we're sliding in the back of a black Sedan, and all my nerves are populating in my knee. It's shaking a million miles a minute; I can't help but be nervous. It feels like I'm losing my virginity all over again. Of course, it doesn't help that that was also with River.

"Are you nervous?" River asks, glancing at my knee.

"Nah," I lie, putting a hand on my leg and willing it to stop.

"There's nothing to worry about." River takes my hand in hers; our fingers connect perfectly. I forgot how well we fit together.

I just smile. I'm not sure what to say, and River's hand in mine is bringing back too many memories. I spiral as I think about feeling her skin on mine and kissing her again. Would it all feel the same, or would all the chemistry we once felt be gone?

"Up here is perfect, thanks," she tells the driver, and we hop out in front of a high-rise apartment building on the Upper East Side. I'm not surprised she's doing well for herself.

River takes my hand, smiles at the doorman, and then leads me into the elevator. She presses the button for the fifth floor as I lean against the back of the elevator and let out a deep sigh. I've had one-night stands before—even in apartments as nice as this. But I've never had a one-night stand with someone who once meant everything to me. I glance over at River. She's standing in front of me, crazy curls all about, her denim skirt teasingly short due to those long legs. God, I remember how good she used to feel. Knowing I'm just a few minutes away from that feels like torture.

River leads me to her apartment that's around the corner from the elevator. After unlocking the door, she steps in and removes her Doc Martens. I follow suit and remove my boots.

"Do you want something to drink? I'm sure I have some wine in here," River says opening the silver fridge door.

"No, thanks."

"Beer?" River picks up a beer and I pause.

"I actually don't drink, anymore," I say awkwardly.

"Oh." River's voice goes up an octave. "Like, ever?"

"Like, ever." I nod.

"Okay, water then? Iced tea?" She mentions more drinks as she puts back the bottle of wine.

"No, I'm okay."

"Okay. I've honestly needed to pee since we were at the concert. I'll be right back." She excuses herself and heads down the hall, and it gives me a second to look around.

Her living room is small; there's a black couch and a TV on a dark wood stand. But the view she has is unreal. Two floor-length windows show off the view of Central Park in the distance. Signs of River are all around the room: her record player next to the TV, the knitted quilt her grandma gave her when she was a kid, and the art of queer women hung on the walls.

"Back, sorry about that." River comes into view and catches me looking around.

"It's a really nice place." I smile.

"Thanks, I just moved in last year, but it's close to my job and I love the view."

Another awkward silence envelops us, so I look at River, who's lost the jean jacket she was wearing and is showing off more skin. Her tube top hangs low on her breasts, and her full sleeves of tattoos are on display now. Her curls are pushed behind her ears, but loose strands peek around her cheeks.

She's gorgeous.

Instead of waiting for her to make the first move, which we both know probably won't happen, I close the distance between us, pull her by the loops of her skirt, and pull her against my waist.

"Oh," slips from River's lips, and I push her curls out of her face. I want to see all of her if we're going to do this. I want to commit every second of this to memory.

I trace my thumb across her cheek and down to her glossy lips. Her breath hitches, and I smile. Even after all this time has passed, she melts under my touch. I lean in to kiss her, our lips brushing gently. A simple peck, then another, and soon my lips are stuck on hers. Her tongue slips into my mouth, and I groan. It's a simple act, but it feels like I've gone so long with her that it's like I'm starving for something I didn't even realize I need.

Our bodies are pressed together as our mouths do all the talking—making up for lost time. Somehow kissing River feels like I'm seventeen again. Our whole lives ahead of us.

Her hands wrap around my shoulders, just like they did earlier tonight when we hugged. I don't know if she felt it, but every nerve ending was on fire from such a delicate touch. Like I was finally back where I needed to be.

"Bedroom," River mumbles between kisses.

"Mmm." I nod.

Not letting go of her, I scoop her body up and her legs wrap around my waist. I cling to her body as she touches my chest. Her hands are dangerously close to my breasts. I have no idea where I'm going, but I'm not pulling away to ask. I open one eye enough to see that, at the end of the hallway, her bedroom door is open. After carrying her to the bed, I gently set her down on the middle of the mattress.

I stand at the edge, my leg between hers while I tear off my T-shirt. I'm glad I wore the cute lace bralette tonight, just in case. Her eyes rack over my chest, and I can tell she's glad I wore it too. I slide my shorts down, and I'm about to pull down my fishnets when River stops me.

"Leave them on," she says, stopping my hand.

I nod and drop to my knees and unbuckle her skirt before sliding it down her deliciously tan and toned thighs. Her pussy is barely hidden by a small red thong. River's eyes are dark with desire, but I want to make sure this is okay, that I'm doing what she wants.

"Is this okay?" I ask, needing her reassurance.

"Yes." She nods. "Please."

That's all I need. I kiss up her thighs, stopping to plant delicate, wet kisses on her inner thighs. It's such a simple act, but I remember it drove her wild all those years ago. A wet spot is forming on her thong, and I can smell her sweet arousal. Stopping to tease her, I brush my face across her pussy, and she gasps at my touch.

"So needy, even after all the time. I can see how bad you want this," I tease.

"Mmm," she hums and nods furiously.

I smirk and slide her dripping-wet panties down her thighs. Her pussy is bare, slicked with desire. I lean down and slip my tongue along her folds, only stopping to give attention to her swollen clit. River gasps and moans under me, her hips bucking against me. God, she tastes just like I remember.

"Please, Aspen," she begs breathlessly.

I swirl my tongue around her clit, sucking on the sensitive bud. She's dripping down my chin, and I love every second of it. Knowing I still turn her on this much—that she still wants me so desperately…

It does something absolutely feral to me.

I run my tongue back and forth between her folds and her clit, soaking up every last drop of her.

"I'm so close," she says desperately.

I don't let up, running my tongue back and forth, just the way she always liked. I allow her body to respond to me, reaching for her breasts. Her nipples are swollen and hard underneath the small tube top. I tug on them, and she moans loudly for me. Just as sensitive as I remembered.

"Oh! Yes! Don't Stop!" River cries out as I pull on her nipple and taste her pussy. She moans and collapses after coming all over my face. This is something I will never grow tired of watching.

"Fuck," I mutter under my breath. I wipe my mouth with the back of my arm and climb onto the bed next to her. My knees are not what they used to be.

"God damn, you always did know how to take me out with your tongue," River praises. "Come here." She pulls me in for a kiss. She's always gone wild for the taste of herself on my lips—and it appears that hasn't changed a bit.

She sucks on my bottom lip and pulls it out enough for me to gasp. She remembers what I like, too. Pulling away, she throws her top across the room and straddles my lap. Her bouncy curls are all over the place, and she looks crazy—but also so fucking hot. Something about her with wild hair always gets me going.

River pushes me onto the bed, head in the pillows, and begins kissing my neck. She stops to suck and lick my collar bone and that spot right behind my ear. Fuck. That little move of hers has always drove me crazy. She nibbles on my earlobe, and I groan. This woman is going to be the death of me.

Her head drops down past my collarbone and to my breasts. Sliding off my bralette over my head, she stops to take a second to appreciate the new piercings I got. She flicks each metal bar with her fingers and then glances up at me.

"Did those hurt?"

"Not any more than you'd expect." I shrug. The pain was worth it for how good they feel when someone plays with them.

"Hmm." She stops to put her mouth on them, and I involuntarily let out a large moan.

"They are fun." She giggles. My nipple is in her mouth and this woman fucking *giggles*? But I don't have a chance to complain because her hand has dropped between us and is running over my panty-covered pussy.

Her hands dance across the fabric of my fishnet tights and then she pulls, roughly.

Riiiiiip.

"Hope these weren't important." She smirks like the devil.

Before I have a chance to speak, she's dropping her head between my thighs and does the same to my panties.

Riiiiiip.

Well, there go my panties. I have only a moment to think about them before she slides her tongue across my pussy, and I decide I don't care about anything else.

5. Joyride

RIVER

I've never had anyone's pussy taste as good as Aspen's. I don't know what kind of diet she's on, but *fuck*. She drips down my tongue, and I'm addicted. She tastes and feels just like I remember. Sure, there are some small changes, like the piercings and the new tattoos. But her body? She's only aged gracefully.

Her legs shake under me as I suck on her clit. She always liked it a little rougher than me. My hand is around her throat as I taste her sweet pussy. Her tights and panties are in shreds. That's something I've never done before, but I just couldn't help myself. I didn't see her complaining once my tongue took over.

"Fuck it. Riv, right there." She groans and pulls on my hair, taking a fistful of my curls and holding me even closer to her pussy.

Stroking her pussy with my tongue, I watch as she comes undone. She falls back onto the bed, and her legs quake under me as her orgasm flows through her body. God, I missed this. I missed how good she looks when she comes for me. I need to attach this to my memory or something because this isn't enough.

"Come here," she commands, and I climb on the bed next to her. She wraps an arm around me, and I kiss her, our lips colliding. At first, it's calm and sweet, but the more we kiss, the more we want.

Our kisses become frenzied, desperate. I don't just want to be kissed, I want to touch her, have her touch me.

"Fuck me," she mumbles between biting my lip and kissing my cheek. Her lips are all over me, and I can't get enough.

She pulls back just long enough to toss off her ripped tights and panties. I smirk, knowing I'll be paying for that later. Aspen pulls me back on top of her and slides a hand between us. Her fingers dance across my clit, teasing me before sliding inside. She curls them deep inside me and I gasp.

"Oh, Aspen!" I cry. Her fingers slide in and out of me like that's where they belong.

"I need you." She moans. Her lips kiss my neck, my collar bone, my lips. She's everywhere and somehow not in enough places all at once.

"How?" I ask as her fingers disappear. I frown, desperate for another release.

"Scissor me," she says.

We position ourselves—she leans back, and I straddle her leg. Our pussies connect, both of us gasping at the contact. Our clits and slick folds collide as we slide back and forth. She holds one of my legs while I hold one of hers, moving at the same rhythm. It did not feel this good when we tried it as teenagers. Clearly, we've learned what to do in our time apart. I ignore the twinge of jealously, thinking about who might have been the one to teach her. I don't have any room to talk; I've been with people too, but for some reason it still hurts.

"Fuck, you feel so good." Aspen moans.

I reach for her chest, playing with her nipples. I flick the metal bar with my thumb and watch as Aspen gasps. She's soaked. Her juices cover my thighs. Our desires mix as our clits brush together. Pulling me closer, she kisses me. This time, it's rough and frenzied. She must be close. Her hand digs into my thigh. I suck on her tongue, and she tosses her head back, starting to moan.

"Oh, fuck me!" Aspen cries out, and I watch as her mouth twists into the most beautiful masterpiece as she comes undone. Her hair falls down her back, and she collapses against the bed.

I run my fingers over my clit and look at Aspen's body. Her perfect breasts, hardened nipples, her glistening pussy—it's all I need to have my own orgasm. She locks eyes with me as I come undone and fall into bed with her. After a few breathless gasps, I come back down.

I grab a scrunchie from my nightstand and attempt to pull my hair into a bun.

"Mmm, I love your hair," she murmurs.

"Well, I'm too hot right now." I laugh.

"We could take a shower?" Aspen raises an eyebrow.

"That actually sounds like a good idea." I nod.

Getting out of bed, I grab a towel from the closet and an extra one for Aspen. She catches it and follows me to the bathroom across the hall. I turn on the water, giving it a second to get warm. I've jumped in too early and froze my tits off so many times. I open the mirror that doubles as a cabinet and pull out some makeup wipes. I hand one to Aspen, and we both take off our eye makeup.

I get in the shower first, pulling the curtain aside so she can climb in. There isn't as much space as I anticipated. Her body is pressed against mine as I look for the bar of soap. Her hands are on my breasts, her breath on my ear while she nibbles on my shoulder. I shiver, her fingers playing with my nipples as I struggle to rub the soap all over my body. Aspen takes it from me, rubbing it down my shoulders, all over my back and my butt. She stops to grab and squeeze, even sliding a hand between my thighs, and I gasp.

"The water will go cold if we start that in here," I warn her.

"This fancy apartment and the water goes cold too quick? Sounds like a challenge." I don't have to look at her to know she's smirking.

Aspen slides two fingers in my pussy. I gasp as she hands me back the soap with her free hand, and I clutch the wall for support.

"Keep getting clean, don't mind me," she murmurs in my ear. It's comical that she thinks I could focus on anything else while her long, thin, fingers are inside me.

"Aspen," I moan out as she reaches around to play with my nipples. The water slides down my soapy chest, and I turn to face her. She readjusts her hand inside me, and the eye contact with her is more intense than I anticipate.

"Come on, Riv. I know you can come faster for me." She smirks and curls her fingers, brushing her thumb across my clit.

"As—" I attempt to moan her name, but she kisses me into silence. I could get lost in her body, but fuck, her tongue does things to me I just can't explain. We're like two teenagers playing with fire.

"Come for me," she whispers against my wet lips. I force my eyes open to look right at Aspen as I come on her hand. Something about that dirty mouth of hers always gets me going.

"That's a good girl." She drags her fingers to her mouth and sucks them dry one at a time. My juices find a home on her tongue.

I push her against the shower wall and kiss her feverishly. I want to soak up every second of this. I don't know how long we're kissing, but the water starts to turn icy, and I jump out. I'm clean enough, and my hair can be washed in the morning. It's too intricate of a process to do now.

"Ah, you can't leave me in here alone!" Aspen cries as she hurries to get clean before it turns to complete ice.

"I'll grab you something to wear!" I call back, laughing.

Wrapped in a warm towel, I head back to my room. Should we wear pajamas? I usually sleep in leggings and a T-shirt, but if our time in the shower was any indication, we won't be keeping clothes on for very long. I decide to grab us both oversized T-shirts and nothing else. If she wants to wear more, I'll find her something. I don't even know if she's actually staying over, but she can't go home in her ripped tights, and she'll at least need a clean pair of panties. I discard her ripped pair into the trash can by my bed and quickly clean up all the clothes and makeup Cari and I had left strewn about.

I toss the shirt over my head and go back to the bathroom where I find Aspen drying off. Her body is dripping. The bathroom is chilly, and her nipples are hardened. Her body is curvier than I remember. Small stretch marks span across her sides from growing taller, I assume. She's older, more mature. The last five years have aged her, but in a beautiful and natural way. Her hair is in a messy bun just like mine, and I love how she looks with it tossed up. There's a small amount of mascara running down her cheeks, some she obviously missed when using the makeup wipe. I step forward to rub it away softly with my thumb. She grabs my wrist and holds it, staring into my eyes.

Neither of us speak. Her hand wraps around my wrist and pulls me closer. I close the distance, placing a small kiss on her lips, but she holds me tight and my body presses against hers. This kiss feels different. Like she's afraid to let me go. Like she's afraid I'm going to pull away. Eventually, she pulls back, letting me go. First my body, then my wrist, and then her eyes fall.

"I-I brought you a shirt." I hold up the grey shirt.

"Thanks." Her hand brushes over mine, and it feels more intimate than I think she intends.

Aspen puts on the T-shirt and follows me back to bed. We're both quiet. I don't know if it's the reality of tonight hitting us or what. But neither of us seem to know what to say next. I don't want her to go, but I'm also afraid of her staying. It's been a while since I've done the whole one-night thing. She climbs into bed next to me, and it's clear she's not going anywhere right now. She rests her head on a pillow, facing me. She reaches out to run her thumb across my cheek, and I shut my eyes, taking in this moment. She traces my cheek, across my lips, and back down my neck.

"Is it cool if I stay?" she asks quietly.

"Yeah, sure." I try to sound cool, nonchalant about it. But I'm sure my desperation is written all over my face. I fell back into bed with my ex, and I'm already regretting it. Not for the obvious reasons. Because it's going to be so much harder when she leaves me again.

"Do you still need TV to fall asleep?" she asks after a few minutes.

For a second, I'm confused. Then I think back to all the nights it was too quiet in my house, and we'd fall asleep with the TV on or her telling me a story. Anything to erase the quiet at night. I've mostly grown out of it, especially with the help of the roaring city sounds around me. But I'm happy she remembers.

"Nah, not so much." I shake my head.

"I guess that's good." She smiles.

I'm not sure what to say, and I'm starting to feel more tired than I was before the shower. Maybe it's the multiple orgasms finally hitting me. My eyes start to close, and the only thing I think and wish, is that Aspen will still be here when I wake up.

6. Pretending

ASPEN

River fell asleep before me last night, and somehow, I'm awake before her. I could blame it on a lot of things, but honestly, it's probably just my nerves. I mean, I hadn't seen River in years, and then we had this earth-shattering night. I think I'm supposed to just get up and leave soon because this is just a one-night thing—not that we ever said it aloud. Still, I'd be stupid to assume it could be anything more.

River breathes quietly in her sleep, and I watch her chest raise and lower slowly. She's dressed in her oversized One Direction T-shirt that she got when she was ten. She's one of the few people who can say they saw the entire band live—and together. It's something that used to get her bragging rights back in the day.

I can't help but smile when I look at her. She looks so peaceful when she sleeps. I woke up entangled in her arms, which was a little difficult to untangle myself from when I had to pee. But now, I wish her arms were back around me. It's barely past seven a.m., and the last thing I want to do is go home at this ungodly hour. I already know I'll have to answer a million questions from my mother. It's not like I'm almost thirty years old or anything. Or heck, maybe she doesn't even know I'm gone. She's been in and out of phases like that lately. I wouldn't put it past her.

River stirs next to me and peeks open one eyeball. I think she's going to freakout or kick me out of her bed, but instead she smiles.

"Let's go back to sleep," she murmurs and pulls me into her arms.

I don't sleep, but the weight of her arm across my waist feels amazing. Her eyes flutter closed almost instantly. I trace her cheek, down her lips, and move back to her cheek over and over again with my thumb. It's like I'm checking to make sure she's real. That *this* is real. I'm in in over my head. There's no way I can have a one-night stand with my ex-girlfriend and just let it be. I guess I can pretend, if that's what she wants. But there's no denying the connection between the two of us.

I play with a loose curl for what feels like forever, rolling the ringlet around my finger and letting it bounce back into place. This used to be my favorite pastime, watching her curls bounce around for me. Hours pass, and around nine-thirty, River finally starts to wake up. I think, at first, she's surprised to see me; I don't blame her. Last night was unexpected, to say the least.

"Good morning." I smile.

"Mmm, good morning." She stretches her arms above her head like a cat. She lets out a loud yawn and then curls into my arms.

"I didn't know if you'd still be here when I got up," she admits quietly.

"I can go if you wan—"

"No, it's okay that you're here." She stops me.

"Last night was fun," I muse.

"*Fun.*" She pauses on the word. "Yeah, it was."

"Do you have work today?"

"Yeah, I usually go in around one on Saturdays," she says.

I don't know what to say; it feels like all the small talk is drying up. I take this as a chance to head out before things become too awkward and she kicks me out or something.

"I should get going. I have some stuff to do on my day off," I say nonchalantly. I get out of bed and begin looking on the floor for my clothes.

"Okay." River sits up in bed and pulls her phone off the charger.

I grab my skirt, my crop top and realize my panties and tights are gone. It isn't like I could wear them anyway. She had ripped them to shreds last night. So, I slide off her T-shirt and put my clothes on. I guess I'll be riding home commando.

"Wait, do you need a pair of panties?" River asks watching me get dressed.

"Oh, nah." I shake my head. It wouldn't be the first time I've gone commando.

"That's kind of hot," River mumbles and bites on her bottom lip. *Fuck.* This woman really is going to be the death of me.

I smirk. "Have you seen my phone?"

"Yeah, you plugged it in over there before bed." She points across the room, and I see it sitting on her dresser. I pick it up and scroll through the notifications. There's nothing that can't wait until later. After slipping my phone into my skirt, I look back at River.

"Lemme walk you out," she offers.

I follow behind her, watching as the T-shirt she's wearing shows off just the edge of her ass as she walks. God damn, I'll miss seeing her body again. I guess there's some things that time can't account for.

River stands by the door, and we both look at each other awkwardly. This feels like more than just a one-night stand, but I don't have it in me to be rejected before ten a.m. I pull on my boots and stand before her.

Then, without thinking twice, I pull River in for a hug, like the one we had last night. Her body presses into mine, and she wraps her arms around my neck. I get a whiff of her sweet shampoo. I desperately need to commit this feeling to memory, so I hold her for as long as she allows me to. I lean in before I can overthink it and press my lips to hers. She's not surprised but welcoming with my kiss. If I had to guess, this is our way of saying goodbye.

"Bye Riv." I wave before heading down the hall to the elevator.

Once the doors shut and I know she isn't running after me like in some cheesy, cliché movie, I let out a sigh. I don't think anything could've mentally prepared me for being with River again. If someone would've told me I'd have spent the last twelve hours in her bed, I would've thought they were joking. Nothing about this was expected, and I'm not even sure how I feel about it all.

Before leaving, I ask the doorman for directions to the subway. Then, a few blocks later, I hop on the train and head all the way back to Queens. I wish I had my headphones. I'm uncomfortable from clenching my thighs together, so I do my best to not think about it and close my eyes. River pops into my head, and I replay last night. Seeing her again, talking to her, hugging her, every last touch and kiss. I want to remember it all forever.

"Spare change?" an unhoused woman asks, but I don't open my eyes. I don't have cash on me, and I'm not in the mood to fight with someone. She scoffs but takes the hint and leaves me alone.

I check all my messages that I've missed, but it's mostly client emails and a few texts from Max and some from our group chat with her roommates. Max's texts are just updating me about hooking up with Cari. Apparently, they really hit it off and she spent the night with her. There's also a drunk text from Liz that I promptly delete. She's had a habit of doing that lately. If she gets too drunk, she asks me to come over, and in the morning she apologizes. I just ignore it at this point. It isn't like I'm ever going to accept the invitation, and at this point, it just feels more awkward acknowledging it.

MAX:

Your friend, or your not friend, Cari, is fucking crazy in the best way

I don't think I've ever been so into someone after one night

Did she put some kinda spell on me?

How did it go with your ex girl?

I decide to text Max back later. I'm almost home, and I don't know what to say. We had sex, but it feels like more—at least to me. I have no idea what River's thinking, though. Not anymore. She used to be someone I knew better than anyone else on the planet, and now she's a stranger to me. I hate it.

Sliding my phone into my pocket, I pull out my key and unlock the front door to my apartment. Well, the apartment I share with my mom. It's a two-bedroom with plenty of space for both of us… mostly. It's typically okay unless we both needed to shower at the same time. The whole one-bathroom thing kind of sucks. I brace myself for whatever mood my mother might be in, but to my surprise, she's not in the living room. I don't move, listening out for a moment and then realizing I don't hear anything.

"Ma?" I call out.

"In here!" she calls back. I follow the sound of her voice toward the kitchen and find her sitting alone at the kitchen table, looking out the window while drinking from her Columbia University mug.

"Everything okay?" I look around. There's no sign of anything broken or on fire. If I didn't know better, I might think she's drinking something other than wine.

"Yeah, I was just having breakfast. I made some eggs, but I burned the bacon." She frowns.

She *cooked*? Now I'm really confused.

"There's some leftovers on the stove."

"Oh, thanks, but I'm not hungry."

"Can you put it away? I'm tired." My mom pushes her long dark hair out of her face and walks toward the living room. I'm still not sure what's in her mug, but it isn't a good sign to see it out. It's my dad's mug, and she rarely uses it.

I put the food in some containers in the fridge before heading upstairs to my room. Then, I grab some fresh clothes and underwear. I'm clean from my shower with River last night, so I don't need to do much. A chill cascades down my spine as I think about her pressed against me, orgasming while the water poured on us both. I take a seat on the edge of my bed and grab my phone. Pulling up Instagram, I look for her account. I'm not sure if it's the same, so I go to Cari's page to find her. Cari is an influencer now, I think, and although she unfollowed me years ago, I've always stayed following her. It felt like my last connection to River. Thankfully, Cari posted some photos from the concert last night and tagged River. Her account is private, which makes sense. River isn't about the social media show that Cari loved.

I'm about to give up when I notice the link to her tattoo page in her bio. Clicking on it, I check out all the tattoos she's done on clients recently. It probably has to be a public page so she can get new clients. She's an incredibly talented artist. I recognize a lot of this work as her original artwork. I click on the button to message her. I don't know what I want to say. Am I going to ask to see her again?

I type up several drafts. In some, I'm asking to see her again, and in others, I'm giving her my number. A few of them just talk about how it was nice seeing her again.

None of them seem like the right vibe, so I ultimately give up. As much as I don't want this to be a one-time thing, maybe it's for the best. I don't want us to have to go through *another* breakup. Maybe our true ending was this one-night stand. Maybe things are better off left how we've left them.

In the past.

7. Guess We Lied

RIVER

"Good morning, Gus." I smile when I walk in the shop with their iced caramel macchiato.

"My savior." They take the cup from me and take a hearty sip. "Ahhh."

"Where's Isla and Rae?" I ask, looking around.

"They had a celebrity client this morning that ran late, so they're both on lunch right now. They should be back in twenty," Gus says looking at their watch.

"Do we know who the celebrity was?" I ask in a hushed tone.

"I think it's that singer that comes in every few months," Gus says with a shrug.

I set my things down behind the desk and shrug off my jacket. I look over the schedule in front of me, noting I don't have any clients yet, but there are some people waiting for a walk-in appointment. I could take those in the meantime. I sip my iced mocha and look at Gus, Isla, and Rae's schedules. It's rare to have a client request two of us at once, but not abnormal. Isla and Rae don't have anyone for a while, so I text them and tell them not to rush back from lunch.

"I can take someone here if you're waiting." I look at the small group of girls in front of me.

"You go!" One of them pushes their friend forward, and they

look nervous. They also look young; I definitely need to check IDs for sure.

"What are you thinking?" I smile.

"Well, we all want to get matching lips tattoos," the one they pushed forward says. She opens her phone and shows me a pretty standard pair of lips.

"Okay, we can definitely do that. I just need to see everyone's identification, and we have forms to fill out." I count six of them and pull out six clipboards with consent forms. They each hand me an ID and grab pens from the cup in front of the computer.

"Are we doing any colors or shading?" I ask.

"Yes, but just red ink outline," one of them says, and I nod.

"Okay. Fill these out, and I'll set everything up."

All of their IDs check out, so I start to put their information into the system. One by one, I have them pay for their tattoo's ahead of time. We've had too many people, especially young people, running out without paying. I head into my room to set up; Gus is already back with their next client. I set up the tray for the first client and then grab all the materials I'll need for the other five girls. This shouldn't take me too long. It'll probably take me longer to clean between each girl than it will to actually do the tattoo.

"Who's up first?" I poke my head out of the room, and one of the girls stands. She swallows hard, and I can tell she's nervous, but the most brave of her friends. The last of their group turned eighteen yesterday, and they've clearly been waiting for this.

"Can my friends watch?"

"Of course." I glance at her paper—no allergies and her name is Carmen.

She waves her friends over, and they huddle in the doorway on the opposite side of where I'm working. I'm glad they know not to crowd me, too many almost-accidents have happened that way. I put the stencil on her wrist where she wants it, and once she approves the placement, I make sure it looks even. The tattoo gun buzzes to life, and I look up to make sure no one is going to pass out. That's happened more than I like to admit. There's something about the sound of the tattoo gun that makes people faint…or vomit.

"Does it hurt?" one of the girls ask Carmen.

"Not really? More like it pinches," Carmen says with a wince.

The girls start asking their friend questions, but I honestly tune them out. Between the sound of the gun, the music playing from my computer, and their questions, there's a lot going on. I focus on the tattoo I'm doing and drown out any other noise.

The lips I'm tracing remind me of the lips I had on me just last night. Aspen pops into my head, her lips on mine. My mind drifts off to her lips on my neck, on my chest, trailing down my stomach. I get a tingle between my thighs, and I clench them tight. I can't be thinking about this right now. I am at *work*. But the more I try to focus on the tattoo, the more I see Aspen's lips and her body and last night replays in my mind.

To be fair, she's been on my mind most of the morning since she left. When she left, I climbed back into bed next to the T-shirt she had been wearing. I don't know why I did it, but it smelled like her, and I slept until my alarm went off. I took a shower, trying to wash her off my skin. But it's hours later, and I can still feel her touch on my body. Aspen is all over me, and as much as I want to forget, a small part of me is relieved to have this memory.

The truth is, after all these years, my memories with Aspen are fading. I could barely remember her voice, let alone her moans and whimpers. But now it's like everything is in HD again. I can see it as clear as day—like a movie. I know that isn't going to help me move on, but a girl can fantasize, right?

The night with Aspen had been unexpected but remarkable. Waking up next to her, it felt like no time had passed. I was half-tempted to ask her to stay. But the words didn't come out, and instead, Aspen disappeared from my life once again. With no way of contacting her, I'm trying to make peace with it. A one-night stand between past lovers. Nothing more.

"Okay, give me a second to clean up, and I'll take whoever's next." I smile.

Carmen's tattoo looks perfect, and she barely bled, which is awesome. I clean her up, wrap the tattoo with second skin, and then clean off the chair and the table. I set up a completely new tray of supplies for whoever is next while Carmen shows off her tattoo to her friends, and they all gush over it. Lily hops into the chair next, handing me the consent form and asking for the placement to be the same as Carmen's.

Once again, I tune everything out. This time, the thought of Aspen between my thighs replays in my mind. I can't help but think about her tongue working circles over my clit, my thighs clenching together. I can still feel her on me. I know she isn't here, but if I were to close my eyes, I might think she is. Of course, I'm currently keeping my eyes open and focused on Lily's tattoo. Aspen's hands are something to write home about. Clearly, I'll be practicing some solo self-care after work, because I need to take care of this itch. Sex with Aspen was always good, but after five years apart, it feels less *good* and more *explosive*. Her fingers and lips were dynamite to my body.

Once everyone's tattoos are done, Isla and Rae pop their heads into my room. I smile when I see them holding the coffee I brought them. I figured they'd find it in the mini fridge by the front desk. Rae takes a seat on the chair near me, her curly blonde hair cascading all over her face, and Isla hangs in the doorway. Her hair, which she dyes frequently, is a white-ish blonde with a bright-pink streak running down the right side. It's cute as hell, definitely not something I could pull off.

"How's it going?" Rae smiles.

"How was the concert last night, you lucky bitch!" Isla teases. LULY is a lesbian icon, and it's no secret. We love her around here, because everyone who works here is part of the queer community.

"It's amazing. She's even better live than I anticipated."

"You could lie to me." Isla rolls her blue eyes.

"I could, but Rae likes to hear the truth." I laugh.

"Fair point, did Cari have fun?" Rae asks.

"She did! She got lots of content and a date out of it."

"Cari got to go to the concert AND she got laid? Unbelievable." Isla scoffs and I laugh. I know Isla isn't as bitchy as she comes across.

"Hey, your three p.m. clients are here," Gus says, poking their head in.

"Whoops, gotta go." Isla, Rae, and I all head to the front of the shop. It's only Isla and Rae who have clients there, so I catch up on the paperwork until we get a walk-in.

"Cari and you have fun last night?" Gus asks after finishing up with their client.

"Yeah." I smile. "We ended up separating later in the night, though."

"Oh, yeah? Did you meet someone?" Gus winks and I laugh.

"Kind of? More like re-met someone."

"Oh?"

"Aspen, my ex, was there. And I sort of went home with her last night. Well, she went home with me technically," I admit in a whisper.

"Shit, how the hell did that happen?"

Gus, Isla, Rae, and I have been friends for almost three years now. We all met at a queer tattooing convention in New Jersey a few summers ago. We decided to keep in touch, and when we all admitted to wanting the same thing—to open an inclusive tattoo shop—we pooled our funds together and became co-owners of RARE's tattoos. We opened the shop on the second floor in a midtown office building a year and a half ago. The shop has become way more successful than we would have ever imagined. And in that time, the four of us grew close. We've come to know a lot about each other's lives, and we consider each other a family. So, Gus is no stranger to the history with Aspen and me.

"I don't really know. We just saw each other, we talked, and then we hugged, and I invited her over. It's like no time had passed, but it's also like we're getting to know each other all over again. It's hard to explain."

"No, that makes perfect sense. You're somewhat strangers, but you also know each other better than so many others."

"Yeah. It's surreal experiencing that."

"Are you going to see her again?"

"Probably not. It felt like a goodbye, and we didn't exchange numbers or anything." I frown.

"Maybe that's for the best. Sometimes a good hookup is all an ex can be good for."

"That's true." I nod.

Gus heads out for their lunch break, and I finish up the paperwork behind the desk. I help a few walk-ins and I try not to think about Aspen. Would things be different had we exchanged numbers? I could always search her on social media, but maybe Gus is right. Things are better left in the past. We're exes for a reason, and I still don't forgive her for how she left me. It wasn't something I felt comfortable mentioning last night, but I'm healed now, and I don't need to fall apart again. Yeah, it's definitely for the best that we didn't exchange numbers.

At least that's what I'm going to keep telling myself.

8. The One

ASPEN

I use my fingers to run up the folds of my dripping pussy. I've been like this for days. No matter what or when, my mind has been on River and the night we spent together. It's like a porno playing over and over in my mind. The sounds River made, the way her body felt, and the way mine reacted to hers. I'm desperate for her touch again, but obviously, I'm settling for my own.

I move my fingers toward my clit, circling the sensitive bud, and then I close my eyes, thinking about River. I replay the other night in my mind while I imagine it's her fingers on me. I've been so pent up lately; I'm sure it won't take long for me to come. My fingers are drenched in my juices, and I want a release. I slide two fingers inside me and pump harder than normal. I'm so close, and I want to get on with my day. I work myself faster and harder, and then I brush my thumb across my clit a few times, and I'm choking back a moan.

Fucking River. I hate the affect she has on me.

Tossing the sheets off my body, I take the rest of my clothes off and head for the shower. I have to meet a client in an hour, and I'll be late if I don't get a move on. After rushing through my shower, I decide to do a no-makeup makeup look. My clients often see me as a background person. So, I don't do anything that might overshadow them, especially on their big day. I grab all my supplies and race out the door. My mom is still sleeping on the couch in front of the television when I leave.

Sighing, I think about asking her if she's given any thought to going to another AA meeting, but I know what she'll say. Living with an alcoholic for most of my life hasn't been easy, and it's almost anything but predictable. Until it comes to this, her same usual speech about not having a problem and being able to quit whenever she wants. It sometimes ends in her going sober for a day or two which are literal hell. Then she goes to the other extreme of binge drinking. One time I couldn't find her for two days, then an officer brought her home and said she had been sleeping in the park. Thankfully, I was already nineteen at that point or CPS might've been called.

I love my mom, I really do, and I understand her drinking is her way of coping with my dad's death. I just wonder what it would've been like if he was still here. It's been over a decade, and my mother just seems to be getting worse, not better. Pushing this out of my head until later, I hop on the subway and pull out my phone.

MAX:
We still on for tomorrow?

ME:
Yes, remind me what time

MAX:
10 a.m. sharp. I only have the space for a few hours

ME:
Got it. I have a wedding today but will be home by 4. All yours tomorrow.

MAX:
Perfect.

. . .

Max is hosting a shoot tomorrow and needs me to do makeup. It's a paying gig, and the photos will be in a few different places, so to have me listed as the makeup artist will be great for my career. Max insists on using me as often as she can. She said it's because of my talent, but I think having me on set makes her a little less nervous. She's talented, but she often doubts her abilities. Not that she ever actually says this out loud, of course.

Looking up at the map on the train, I realize my stop is next. I pop out my headphones and make sure I have everything. The subway lets me off two blocks from the hotel, and I head straight to the bridal suite like the bride told me.

Once there, I knock on the door.

"Who is it?" a voice calls.

"Aspen Wheeler. I'm the makeup artist," I call back, and the door opens.

"Oh, you're early! Feel free to set up wherever. My hairstylist is almost done with everyone, and then you can start." The bride, Bella smiles. She's the one I met for the trial run. She's quite specific about what she wants.

I nod and take a spot by the mirrors. Unpacking all my supplies, I look at the bridesmaids. They all have different skin tones, but I have everything I need. It's a small wedding party of only three—plus the bride. Of course, the other bride has her own makeup artist for her and the party as well. They had wanted me to do both, but I thought it would be a better idea for them to each have their own so there was no crossover or concern on time. Thankfully, they agreed with me.

"Ellie, can you go first?" Bella asks her pink-haired friend.

"Sure." She nods and plops in the chair in front of me. "Hi, I'm Ellie."

"Aspen." I smile and shake her hand.

"You gotta make me look hot, because my girlfriend is here," Ellie announces loudly.

"Ellie, will you let her do her job?" The brunette friend of hers laughs.

Ellie fidgets more than I'd like, but I'm used to antsy clients. Every, once in a while I get a nervous bride, too. She talks to her friends, acting as if I'm not here. I'm used to that, too, and truthfully, it doesn't bother me. I'm just here to make them look even prettier; I don't need to put effort into the conversation. Besides, sometimes listening and not speaking gets me some of the best gossip. Especially when it comes to the New York socialite types. I can't remember what Bella does for a living, but I know her future wife runs a publishing house here in the city.

"Ellie, can you button me up? I want to make sure they're done right," Bella asks once Ellie is done with her makeup.

"I promise I won't skip a button. I did make the dress, after all." She laughs.

"You made the dress?" I ask, my jaw dropping. It's a beautiful white wedding gown, that clings tightly against Bella's body. The white satin fabric hangs off her shoulders and is buttoned down low to her butt. It's a beautiful dress, and I'm even more impressed to know her best friend made it.

"I did. I'm a designer when I'm not this one's bridesmaid," Ellie teases.

"Hey! You act like I get married often; this is only my first wedding." Bella scoffs.

"It's very impressive," I muse. "I have a friend who's a professional photographer, and they would love the chance to shoot a designer they know personally."

"I'd love that; are they queer? I'm always looking to work with more queer and under-appreciated artists."

"Yes, Max is about as gay as they come. I'll give you her card when I'm done." I smile.

"Perfect."

I start on her friend Morgan's makeup while the other girls fawn over Bella and take some candid shots with the photographer. I didn't even notice when they came in the room. Morgan's makeup takes a little longer than Ellie's because it takes some time to get the shade to match her light skin tone. But once I do, she looks as beautiful as her friend.

"Hey, I'm Reagan. Twin sister of the bride. So you have to make me look even better than her."

"I heard that!" Bella laughs from across the room.

I laugh, happy about the light and friendly environment. There's no stress or animosity. Everyone is happy to be here and happy to stand alongside Bella. It's a refreshing change from the drama and stress I often see at events like this. Everyone is sipping on champagne, talking about how happy they are for Bella and Dylan, and gushing over how beautiful she looks. They're all wearing matching light-green bridesmaid dresses that somehow make them all look hot. I've never seen dresses that look that good on everyone involved, especially bridesmaid dresses. I always thought it's a joke to make your friends look terrible so you look better on your big day.

I finish Reagan's makeup, and Bella sits in the chair. I grab the cape I bring in case of emergencies and drape it over her beautiful dress. The last thing I want is to drop eyeliner over her lap and ruin the wedding.

"When you're done with my makeup, you should help yourself to a cocktail." Bella smiles.

"Thanks, but I don't really drink." I shrug.

"Gotcha. Well, there's sparkling water and juice, too."

My phone starts blowing up with messages from Max, and I'm not sure what she wants. I'm about to put my phone on *do not disturb* but she calls me. It's a bit out of character for Max. She doesn't call often, especially when she knows I'm at work.

"Can you give me a minute?" I ask Bella.

"Go for it, we've got plenty of time."

She waves me off, and I step into the hall to answer it.

"Max?"

"Oh, thank god you answered. I'm low-key freaking out," she exclaims, which sounds less low-key than I thought.

"What's going on?"

"My model for the shoot canceled for tomorrow! And now I don't know what to do because the agency doesn't have anyone else that's free, and I don't know what to do. I even asked Liz and Rachel but they both have work they can't miss," Max explains in a long-winded explanation.

"Okay. Lemme think." I pause.

"Okay." Max sighs. Light footsteps sound hurried in the background, and I imagine her pacing in her room.

"What about Cari? Could you ask her?" I don't know if they exchanged numbers or what after hooking up, but I could track her down if Max needed.

"She's doing social media for the shoot, she'll be behind-the-scenes on set. But wait, maybe she knows someone who would do it."

"Yeah, maybe." My head immediately thinks of River, but I don't know if she'd do it. It doesn't seem like her kind of thing.

"Let me make some calls."

"Okay, I'm at work so just text me updates."

"Shit. I'm so sorry. Go kick ass!" Max hangs up and I smile. I'm sure Cari can help out in some way. I assume Cari has tons of friends who would kill to be a model for a day.

I head back into the room, say a quick apology to Bella, and get started on her makeup. Everything looks amazing by the time I'm done, so I take a few quick photos of my masterpiece. Bella and her friends all head downstairs while I clean up. Sometimes I wish I could see the actual wedding, especially on days like today when Bella and her wife-to-be actually seem happy.

Alas, I need to be up early tomorrow, and I don't want to get behind on anything. I steal a sparkling water on my way out and catch a glimpse of the other bride. She's a good decade older than Bella, but I'd be lying if I said she's not hot too. I let them go first, waiting for the elevator behind them, and then I catch the subway home. Max doesn't text me any updates, so I have no idea what's going on with the model fiasco, but I'm too afraid to ask. I don't want Max losing money on this if she can't find someone else to do the shoot. I feel bad, and I really hope she can find someone.

I try not to think much about it, though, because anytime I think about reaching out to someone…I think about River, and how I'd love to reach out to her.

9. Feel

RIVER

Cari sits on the edge of my bed while I stare at her like she has ten heads.

"You want me to be a *model*? Have you lost your mind?"

"I know it's not typically your thing, but it's not like you have to be a real model for this shoot. Max is shooting real looking people," Cari pleads.

"And Max thought to ask me?" I look at her with an eyebrow raised.

"No, she's currently freaking out because all her friends are busy, and she needs someone."

"Why can't you do it?"

"Because I already pitched the idea of doing a behind-the-scenes of a photo shoot to my content manager, and they loved it. So if I do it then I can't be behind-the-scenes getting what I need," Cari explains.

I sigh. "Well, what exactly does it entail?"

"Technically, you have to wear some lingerie and just pose with the male model. But it can be as spicy as you want. She's going for authentic."

"She knows I'm a lesbian, right? How is it going to look authentic?" I scoff.

"Yes, but I don't know. You can pretend he's a woman or something."

"I don't know." I frown.

"Please? I promised Max I'd find someone, and I thought you'd be perfect for it. You're beautiful and you wear lingerie as going out clothes sometimes."

"I guess that's true."

"I just feel bad for Max. She rented out this space and everything, and the model she hired bailed last minute. She's saying she's sick while also posting from a cruise ship." Cari rolls her eyes.

"Alright, I'll do it." I pause. "Wait, is Aspen going to be there?"

"No, why would she be?"

"I don't know." I frown. I can't tell whether I'm disappointed or not.

"I'll text you all the details, but we can go together. We have to be there tomorrow by 10 a.m. Are you working tomorrow?"

"Yes, but I'm sure I can have someone cover it." I pull out my phone and send a text to the group chat. Almost immediately everyone tells me they can cover me and not to worry.

"Perfect, let me call Max. She'll be so relieved!" Cari steps out of my room to make the phone call.

I lie back on my bed and sigh. What the hell do I know about being a model? Nothing. But I guess it'll be a good promo opportunity for the shop. I could have them tag my tattoo account instead of my personal one. Gus and Isla did most of my tattoos anyway; it's a good opportunity to mention that.

"Okay, Max says she loves you forever." Cari smiles as she walks back in. She frowns when she sees me. "What's wrong?"

"I don't know. I'm not the biggest fan of being in front of the camera." I sigh.

"Maybe this will be good for you, get you out from behind the shadows."

"I guess." I sit up. "So what's going on with Max?"

"What do you mean?" she asks coyly.

"You know what I mean. You guys exchanged numbers?" I raise an eyebrow.

"We did." She nods.

"Cari, I have never known you to get a woman's number after a one-night stand. Are you telling me this might be more than a one-time thing?"

"I-I don't know." She blushes.

"Oh my god! You totally like Max."

"I like getting to know Max, and yes, she has an incredible tongue. But that doesn't mean I'm suddenly going to settle down and date someone."

"Uh huh. I give it three months and I'll be hearing wedding bells."

"No way. I doubt I'll ever get married, and I'm sure Max feels the same." She waves me off like I'm crazy.

"Sure." I laugh.

"What about you and Aspen, huh? You've been avoiding that topic all week."

"There's nothing to tell." I shrug.

"Liar!" she exclaims.

"We hooked up, but we didn't exchange numbers or anything. So I doubt we'll see each other again."

"Don't be so sure about that." Cari smirks. I raise an eyebrow about to ask what she means but she just shrugs. I hate when she acts all mysterious like that.

♥♥♥

Cari and I arrive on the photo shoot set by nine forty-five a.m. She wanted to be early, just in case, and I had no choice but to follow my best friend. I have knots in my stomach and could barely eat the croissant and iced coffee I got on the way. Still, I choked it down, not wanting to have to stop the photo shoot for a snack break. Do models get snack breaks? Am I considered a model? Cari seemed to think so.

"Thank you SO much for coming!" Max exclaims when she notices us. She's wearing all-black, and she has a large camera lens in her hands. Her hair is slicked back like James Dean, and I notice a small tattoo behind her ear.

I glance behind her and notice the set is a bedroom. There's a large canopy bed in front of a huge window with a view of Midtown Manhattan. The bed is covered in red satin sheets. Even though I can't feel them, I can only assume they're soft. There are rose petals on the floor near the bed along with a bottle of champagne and two glasses.

"We're going for a romantic vibe. You and your partner are having a romantic encounter, and you're making the most of the night you have together. It's supposed to be sexy and intimate. Two lovers, if you will," Max explains.

"Lovers with a stranger?" I wince. I don't know if I can do this.

"Yes, but you'll love Greg. He's also gay, so trust me you'll feel safe. And if at any point you want or need to stop, just yell and I'll shut everything down. I want my models to feel comfortable here." Max smiles, reaching out to squeeze my hand.

"Okay." I nod.

"Any questions?"

"Do I get to meet Greg? Like before the shoot?"

"Yes, he should be here any minute. I'll have someone bring you clothes to choose from. They are all brand-new, and they're your size, according to Cari. Then Aspen will do your hair and makeup." Max smiles.

"Aspen?" My voice gets caught in my throat, but Max has already walked away. I look back at Cari, but she's talking to an assistant about lighting.

I thought Aspen wasn't going to be here. Now she's not only going to be here, but she's also doing my hair and makeup. Then, she'll be watching me get intimate with some guy. This all feels like too much. I don't want to bail and leave Max in a bigger predicament than before, but I don't know what to do. I take a seat on one of the benches and try to focus. Cari must sense my distress and runs to my side.

"Hey, you good?" She looks at me with her brows furrowed.

"Yeah, no. I thought Aspen wasn't going to be here."

"I didn't know. Max didn't say anything."

"Okay."

"You've seen her before. Just act normal. She's not going to be weird if you aren't."

"That's true." I nod. Okay, just act normal. I can do that.

"River? Here are all the clothes to choose from." An assistant with blonde hair walks the rack over to me. I almost laugh at their idea of *clothes*; this stuff will barely cover my body.

"Do I just have to pick one?"

"Actually, we're going to do at least one change. So Max said to pick your top three." She smiles.

"Okay." I walk through the clothes, playing with the fabric between my fingers and trying to see which one will make me feel most confident and most like myself.

"I love that one." Cari smiles as I pick out a black bodysuit. It's lacy and covers the main parts but shows enough skin to make it sexy.

"This is my first choice," I tell the assistant. She nods and takes the hanger from me.

I grab two more—both purple. One is a bodysuit, and one is a two-piece. They're a little more scandalous, but I think I can rock them. I wore less clothing to Pride in the past. I just need to be in the right mindset for it. I hand the last choices to the assistant who says she's going to put them in the dressing room for me, then I nod and glance over the rack of clothes to see the doors open. The light shines through the space, and suddenly, I see Aspen. Dressed in a white T-shirt and ripped black jeans, she somehow looks casual but also sexy as hell. She closes the doors behind her, walks in, and sees me. She offers a vague half-smile that doesn't tell me what she's thinking, and then she beelines for Max.

"Come on, let's get you ready." Cari pushes me toward the dressing rooms.

"I can dress myself, you know."

"I know, but I also need content. Just pretend I'm not here." Cari waves me away. I step into the makeshift dressing room, which is just a chair, a mirror attached to the wall, and a curtain.

I start getting undressed and look over my naked body in the mirror. I'm thankful I just had everything waxed. There isn't a hair on my body—aside from my head. I place my folded clothes neatly on the chair and then look at the lingerie. I can do this; it's nothing. I put on the black bodysuit and then look in the mirror. Damn, I look kinda hot.

"Coming in!" Cari announces and inserts herself into the room. "Damn, you look smoking. I'd hate to be your ex."

"Cari!" I laugh. There's a satin robe hanging on the wall, so I slide it on and tie it closed around my waist.

"Okay, interview time. I know you hate video, so we can do this podcast-style." She holds out her voice memo app.

"Okay." I nod.

"How do you feel being here today? Are you nervous about your first time being on a set?"

"I'm extremely nervous, but I'm also kind of excited. It's not every day I do this kind of thing, so I'm pushing myself out of my comfort zone. And I'm happy to be helping a friend."

Cari asks me a few more general questions before someone is calling us to do my hair and makeup. It's time to face Aspen. But when I walk back to set, Max is on the phone fuming. Cari leaves my side to find out what's going on. I take a seat in the hair and makeup chair and Aspen looks up from her set up.

"Hey," she says softly.

"Hi." I smile. I ignore the way my stomach flips when she looks at me.

"So, Max said she wanted a natural look but one that will still pop on camera. So it's going to look darker than you're used to, but it's so the photos come out better," Aspen explains.

"Okay." I nod.

Aspen glances at Max and Cari, who seem to be having a heated discussion.

"Do you know what's going on?" she asks.

"No idea." I shake my head.

Aspen picks up the flat iron and begins going over my curls with it. It's not often I straighten my hair, but when I do, I always get compliments. She takes her time, picking up small pieces at a time and running the flat iron across them. I can feel her fingertips graze my scalp softly. Aspen glances at me through the mirror in front of us.

"I didn't know you'd be here," Aspen says quietly.

"I didn't either."

"Max and I work together a lot when we can. It helps get my name out there," Aspen says.

"I'm just filling in; the real model couldn't make it."

"Oh." Aspen nods.

Max and Cari walk over, both with stressed and pained expressions on their faces.

"What's going on?" Aspen puts down the flat iron.

"I'm afraid we're going to have to cancel the shoot." Max sighs.

"What? Why?" Aspen asks.

"Greg has the flu, and I can't possibly get another male model this quickly." Max frowns.

"Oh." I was sort of looking forward to it at this point.

We're all quiet as we try to come up with some kind of a solution.

"Does it have to be a male model?" Aspen asks.

"What? Uh, no I guess not. Why? Do you know someone?" Max looks at her confused.

"Well, if you need someone, I guess I could do it. If River's not technically a model, then you don't need real models for it. Right?" Aspen suggests. My eyes follow her to Max who looks shocked.

"Holy shit. You're so right. Making this shoot sapphic might even be the thing to put it over the edge." Max grins widely.

"My followers would love to see more sapphic content," Cari chimes in.

"Is it alright with you?" Aspen turns to me. Cari and Max all look in my direction, but what can I possibly say?

"Of course." I smile. What's the harm in doing a sexy photo shoot with my ex?

10. Her Body is Bible

ASPEN

Cari takes over doing River's hair so I can do her makeup and then get started on my own. Max is busy setting up the shoot for us. River and I haven't said a word to each other since she accepted me co-modeling with her. I wish I had a second to talk to her alone, just to make sure she really is okay with this. I know her, she's going to say she's fine because she doesn't want to upset the team, but I don't want her feeling uncomfortable.

"Am I just straightening her hair?" Cari breaks the silence.

"No, Max wants curls too. My curling iron is in my bag." I point to the bag on the table and Cari nods.

River puckers her lips so I can get the lipstick stain on, and I blush. Something about her and those lips always do it for me. It doesn't help that, from where I'm standing, I can see her breasts if I look down. Her robe is coming undone in the front, and I can see the tops of her peach skin against some black lace. I'm already clenching my thighs together from the thought of seeing her in that and not being able to do anything about it. I have to quietly remind myself this is for Max, my best friend who would do anything for me.

I finish up River's makeup, and then I stand in front of the mirror to do my own. Max gave me full control, but I do it similar to River's so it looks more cohesive for the shoot. Then, I saunter off to find

Max and figure out what the hell I'm about to be wearing. Max is standing next to her two assistants when she sees me.

"Thank you so much for doing this," Max says, pulling me aside.

"Don't mention it, just tell me what I have to wear."

"So, we can totally style you in lingerie similar to River's. Or, we could style you in the clothes meant for Greg." Max waits for my answer.

"What was Greg meant to wear?"

"Boxers."

"What if I wear the boxers and the T-shirt I'm wearing?" I negotiate.

"Can you ditch the bra?" Max asks, looking me over.

"Yeah." I nod.

"Done. Go for it." Max smiles and pats me on the shoulder.

I head to the dressing rooms to get changed. I honestly wouldn't have minded the lingerie, but I'm not exactly shaved down there, and while I don't mind that during sex, it isn't the look I want to share with the public. I ditch the bra and notice how chilly it is in here, my nipples hardening almost automatically. I pull down my blonde hair from the messy bun it's in, and it covers my chest completely—for now. I head back to set, and River is standing in her robe, talking to Cari and Max. Her long legs are on display, and her tattoos are exposed.

"Okay, so we'll just start with whatever feels natural. The original theme of the shoot started off with the couple kissing. Now, I know you guys are exes so there's absolutely no pressure to do that. But if you could look like a couple for at least a few photos I'd appreciate it," Max adds with a chuckle.

River looks more nervous than I've ever seen her, but I nod for Max's sake.

"Do we, um, have to get naked?" River asks, and I almost choke on the air I'm breathing.

"If you feel like taking anything off or having stuff taken off you, by all means. But definitely no pressure or expectations," Max replies professionally.

"If there are no more questions, then River, you can drop the robe when you're ready and we'll get started," Max instructs.

"You'll be great," Cari whispers to her best friend. River drops the robe and hands it to Cari, who places a kiss on her cheek and steps into the background of the shoot.

My eyes drop to River's body and take in her curves, her soft skin, and the way her ass is basically hanging outside of that bodysuit. I inhale a sharp breath. This is going to be a challenge. All I want to do is walk across the room and ravage her...take her on the bed and not care who's watching. But I can see how tense she is and how she must be worried. So I try to help, walking toward her and putting my hand on her shoulder. Max isn't shooting yet; she's still getting everything into place, so it gives us a second.

"Hey," I say quietly.

"Hi." She smiles but doesn't look at me.

"I can't tell if you're nervous because of me or the camera."

"Both," she admits.

"It might go faster if we pretend it's not there."

"Okay." She finally looks at me. Her dark-brown eyes gaze into mine as she takes a deep breath.

I reach for her hand and interlock it with mine. It feels so familiar, but I remind myself this isn't real. None of what's about to happen is real. I walk her over toward the bed. She looks nervous, like I'm about to push her onto it or kiss her or something, but I'm not.

"Look at me," I tell her, and she looks at me again. "If you're nervous or scared, just focus on me. We can pretend it's just us. Like the other night."

"Okay." She nods and this time she actually looks less nervous.

Max starts taking photos, and I can see River about to tense up, so I mouth, "Look at me." Her eyes lock with mine, and I reach to push her curls out of her face. Half because Max probably can't see her face right now, and partially because I'm desperate to touch her. Her face relaxes in my hand, and I smile at her. River's body relaxes, and I step closer to her. I place one hand on her waist, playing with the lace on her hip. The other I trail around her cheek, across her lips, and down her neck. I pull back just before her chest and watch as her breath changes. She's anticipating my touch.

River steps closer to me, and I can smell the scent of her shampoo, her lilac perfume, and the fact that she recently brushed her teeth. Her dark lips pucker, as if she's hesitating. Her eyes dart to my lips, and I know what she's looking for. I know she wants to kiss me as bad as I want to kiss her. I suppose I could help her out, close the distance. But instead, I don't. If she really wants it, she'll have to ask for it.

"Ask me," I say quietly. I don't know if Max is taking photos; I've tuned her and everyone else out.

"Will you kiss me?" she whispers, knowing exactly what I meant.

I don't answer, but I press my chest to hers. Her breath hitches, and I press my lips to hers. Closing my eyes, I lean into the moment. Forgetting where we are and how we're dressed. All I want in this moment is to have River. Is to *kiss* River. Her tongue slips in my mouth while my grip tightens on her waist. She doesn't hold back. She's kissing me just like the other night. Her hands eventually roam to my chest, taking one breast in her hand through my thin T-shirt, and I moan in her mouth. Fuck. The way River makes me come undone so easily...I've never felt this way with anyone else.

When we finally stop kissing, just long enough to get some air, I remember where we are. Max is taking photos, but Cari is blushing and looking on impressed. River starts to look nervous again, but I pull her face toward me. She instantly relaxes, and I take her hand again, this time leading her to the side of the bed.

"Hop on," I instruct, and she sits on the edge of the bed.

I look at her with hooded eyes, a million dirty thoughts racing behind my brain. Instead of talking, I think about the camera on us and what might look good. What might look *real*. So I push River back into the bed, her curls splaying all around her. She lifts one arm over her head and the other at her side. I nudge her thighs open with my leg and stand between them. She looks up at me expectantly. Max has moved from where she's been to get a better angle of us, so she's closer than before but still far enough away that this feels intimate.

I push my hair to one side, opposite of the camera, and then I lean down and begin kissing River's neck. Slowly, I place moist kisses. Pressing my lips under her earlobe, on her neck, then down her chest. Her breathing picks up as I get closer to her breasts, and my other hand steadies my body on the bed.

"Can I?" I motion to her chest, and she nods.

I run my tongue along the curves of her breasts, watching as her breath hitches when my tongue comes in contact with her skin. I can tell she's holding back a moan. Whether it be for me or the audience, I'm not sure. My hand slides up the sides of her waist, up her stomach, and I grab her breasts. Her nipples peak through the thin lace, and I mentally groan. This is going to be the death of me. I look at River, unsure of how far she wants me to go.

"Kiss me," she mumbles quietly, catching my eye.

I nod, climbing halfway onto the bed. She leans closer to me, and I reach to put my hand around her neck. That's not usually her thing, but she seems to be into it for the moment. My hand tightens, and her mouth opens slightly. I can only imagine what this looks like, because god, she looks so gorgeous under my touch.

I press my lips to hers in a haze, our tongues tangling together. My body collides with hers. Our hips grinding together. A moan slips from my mouth to hers, and she smiles. I pull back just for a second, but she's already pulling me toward her. I fall into the bed with her, and she locks her legs around my waist. In a quick maneuver, she's on top of me. *Fuck.* River tosses her hair back and grinds her thighs on my lap. She straightens her back, holding onto the bed with one hand behind her and the other around my neck.

She tightens her grip on me, and I groan. I don't give a shit who hears, because this is fucking hot. I grab her breasts, this time pulling down the lace to expose one breast. Before Max can grab a photo, I slide it in my mouth. That's all for me. All *mine*. I flick my tongue over her nipple, and she gasps. I cover her back up and then do the same to the other side. Thank fuck I'm wearing boxers, because if I was in lingerie like River, I'd be dripping down my thighs with how wet I am. Speaking of, I pop her nipple out of my mouth, careful to cover her up again. Then I run my hand down her chest, keeping eye contact with her as my hand dips below her waist.

River stops me with her hand before I can touch her sweet center. I smirk. She must be soaked if she doesn't want me to check. Or maybe she's afraid of how far this might go with an audience. I can't say I blame her. Half of me forgot there was anyone else here. With these silky sheets and the goddess on my lap, who could blame me?

11. Girls girls girls

RIVER

Aspen's hand almost dips into my center, and I stop her at the last second. The last thing I need are the camera and my best friend seeing me get fucked by my ex. Her hand in that area is a dangerous thing, especially considering how wet I am. I didn't anticipate it getting this hot between us, but once we start going it's hard to stop. The chemistry between the two of us is undeniable; I just hope the camera is seeing that. Max isn't giving us any pointers or critiques, so I assume we must be doing something right. I'm a bit more rigid than I would've been if Aspen and I were alone. But it's hard to forget my best friend is twenty feet away, watching the whole thing.

"Look at me," Aspen whispers from under me. I'm getting distracted again, but she seems to know how to pull me out of that. Something about looking at her made me calm down.

She leans in to kiss me again, but just as our lips are about to touch, Max yells "Stop!"

Aspen and I pull apart, looking at Max. But neither of us move.

"Can I get some shots of you two standing up in front of the mirror? I think it would look really cool."

"Sure." We both nod. I slide off Aspen's lap, and her thigh hits my center, causing me to yelp. I wasn't expecting contact. I'm like a firecracker ready to be set off with a single touch.

"Sorry." Aspen smirks, knowing exactly what she did.

Fine, two can play at that game.

Max points us toward the mirror and then positions herself where she won't be seen. I lean against it, my ass on the cool glass. Aspen stands before me, so I pull her in by her T-shirt—the very thin T-shirt that is just begging to come off. Her nipples could cut through this glass, I'm sure. I tug her toward my waist, and she kisses me.

Our lips melt into each other's, and I wrap my arms around her neck. Her hands find my ass, grabbing and squeezing each cheek. We kiss for a while, until I pull back and whisper in her ear.

"Can I take off your shirt?" She raises an eyebrow and nods.

She takes a small step back, and I take my time pulling the thin fabric over her head. She exhales as I blow a cool breath over her chest. I dip my head, running my tongue on the outside of her piercings and teasing her slowly, watching as she comes undone with my touch. Aspen leans on me for support as I reach for the other breast with my hand. I play with both of them at the same time, knowing just how sensitive she's always been. We've had many times when nipple play alone was enough to make her orgasm for me.

She glares down at me, knowing exactly what I'm doing. Then, she takes my hands and holds them over my head. She presses her chest against mine, and I suck in a breath.

"Don't think I don't know what you're doing," she whispers in my ear.

I just smile, saying nothing. Her lips crash into mine, still holding my hands over my head. I'm not escaping this so quickly. Aspen pulls away and bends down, and as I'm about to ask what she's doing, she places two hands under my ass and lifts me up. My body against the mirror, she holds me on her waist and presses her lips against mine.

Well, fuck. Who knew she could do that?

Aspen kisses me fiercely, and I know it's not for show anymore. I have no idea what today is, but there's no way it's just for the shoot. She grips my ass, and my legs are wrapped around her waist; I'm shocked at how strong she is. But she doesn't waver, my body wiggling against hers. I hope to hell Max and everyone can't see how wet I am, because it's embarrassing at this point. My thighs are soaked, and I'm going to be spending a lot of time with my vibrator when I get home.

"Mmm," Aspen hums against my neck as she nibbles lightly.

I play with her nipples as she kisses me, and I silently wish we were alone right now. I don't know how long it's been, but the foreplay is now crossing into torture territory. I close my eyes and feel everything at once. Her fingers on my skin, her lips on my neck, our bodies pressed against each other's. I let out a small moan in Aspen's ear, and she smiles against my skin. I want her to keep touching me.

"Hello! Aspen! River!" Max's voice next to us makes us both jump, and Aspen drops me.

I fall to the floor with a thud and wince. I don't know if it's more embarrassing or painful.

"Are you okay?" Aspen drops to my side to help me up.

"I'm good, maybe bruised my ass a bit," I joke. It hurt, but only for a second. Knowing how easily I bruise, I probably will have a nasty one tomorrow. Well, at least the photo shoot is today; no one else will be looking at my ass this week.

"I'm sure we can go grab you some ice." Max looks concerned. I wave her off.

"Nah I'm sure I'm okay," I say, standing up.

"We're, uh, done for the day. I definitely got what I needed, and we need time to clean up the set," Max explains.

My cheeks overheat so I just nod.

"Thank you both so much for your help. You really saved my ass today," Max praises.

Cari runs over and pulls me away from Max and Aspen.

"Girl! What is going on?! That chemistry was wild," she whispers to me.

I glance back at Aspen, who's staring at me while Max is talking to her. Her eyes don't leave mine, and she smiles. I smile back, not sure what else to do, and then I look at Cari.

"I-I don't know. I was nervous and then I just wasn't."

"Well, it's hot as hell. Look at this." She opens her phone and clicks on a video of Aspen and me. We're on the bed, kissing and grinding. It looks like the beginning of a porno. A really good and *classy* one.

"Holy shit." My cheeks darken again.

"Don't be embarrassed; it's hot as fuck. Max said she never gets that kind of intense chemistry with her models. She got a ton of amazing photos." Cari smiles.

"Well, that's good."

"Why don't you go change, and we can get some lunch?"

"Sure." I nod.

I head over to the makeshift dressing room. It's the first time I'm alone with my thoughts. What the hell is going on with Aspen and me? Was it really just for show? Am I really expected to just go out there and grab lunch with Cari? How the hell can I not say something to Aspen? Especially after that. But what am I even supposed to say?

Hey, I know you broke my heart by leaving years ago, but the sex is really hot.

Christ.

I feel so desperate. I'm not this girl. I don't crumble and fall back to my exes. But it feels different—Aspen *is* different. I sit on the chair and take a second to think it through. Maybe I shouldn't do anything rash right now, especially considering how turned-on I am. What's that saying…you shouldn't make decisions about life if you're horny, tired, or hungry? I think I'm three for three at the moment.

"Hey, I think I left my pants in there," Aspen says, breaking me free from my thoughts.

"Uh, what?" I look around the empty dressing area and frown. There weren't any pants here.

The curtain opens, and I gasp, jumping up. Although, it really doesn't make any sense considering everyone here already saw me in this outfit. I never even got to change into another one.

"What are you doing in here?" I ask in a hushed voice. Aspen closes the curtain behind her, smirks, and pulls me in for a kiss.

It's softer than before, more intimate and thoughtful. I fall into her arms and melt into her body.

"Wait! What are we doing?" I put my hand on her chest to hold her back. Her T-shirt is back on, and her peaks are poking through.

"I saw how wet you got when I was barely touching you. I thought we might see what would happen if I actually touched you." She winks and I bite down on my bottom lip. As much as I want to say no, there is a thrill in getting caught. In knowing someone could hear us and stop us at any second.

"Touch me," I command, knowing she's waiting for me to say yes.

"Thank fuck," she mutters before sliding a hand between my thighs.

I gasp as her hands touch my pussy.

"Fuck, Riv. You are *drenched*." She slides two fingers through my slick folds and then pulls away. She brings her fingers to her mouth, and I watch as she licks them clean.

"We don't have time for teasing," I grumble.

"Oh, we always have time for teasing."

Aspen drops to her knees, flicking open the bottom of the lingerie, and presses her tongue against my center. I moan, gripping her long blonde hair in my fingertips. Her tongue flicks against my clit, before sliding up and down my pussy. I clamp my free hand over my mouth in an attempt to be quiet, but I know it's pointless. Our friends couldn't be more than fifty feet away and they know exactly what we're up to. Only instead of embarrassing me, it fuels my fire.

"Oh, Aspen." I moan into my hand.

She flicks her tongue over my clit and reaches for my breasts. I undo the straps of my lingerie and let my breasts free for her. She fingers my nipples, hardening them with her touch. Her tongue is heaven and hell all at once. I'm dripping down my thighs, so she keeps stopping to lick me clean. Not allowing even one drop to be missed.

Tugging on her hair, I push her face back against my pussy, and she hums against me. I can feel my orgasm rising. My breathing grows faster and deeper, and her tongue focuses solely on my clit. Aspen slides two fingers inside me, curling them, causing me to buck into her. I groan, probably a little too loud, and I close my eyes. She's killing me. I need to come so fucking bad. Hard and fast, right now. I need to scream her name.

She picks up the pace, swirling circles with her tongue around my clit and pumping her fingers in and out of me.

"Oh, yes," I mumble.

Aspen opens her eyes to look at me. She adds a third finger, and with a flick of her tongue, I'm coming for her.

"Oh, Aspen!" I call out way too loudly. There is definitely no denying what's happening in here, but I don't care. I need her.

I ride out my orgasm on her hand and pull her to my lips to kiss me, savoring the taste of myself on her lips. I tear off her shirt, and my hands are like magnets to her chest. She shrugs out of her boxers and stands naked before me. I don't know how much time we have left, but we have to make it count.

12. Shh...Don't Say it

ASPEN

Watching River come for me as loudly as she did is now a core memory in my mind. The way my name slipped off her lips like it was meant to. I didn't expect to get to hook up with her today, but I refuse to let the chance slip away. She soaked my thigh when I picked her up, so I know how badly she wants me.

Standing naked before River doesn't feel daunting. She's looking at me with desire in her eyes, and I wait for her to make the next move. She drops to her knees and looks up at me with bold eyes as she pouts. Her lips pucker, and I swear she's trying to kill me. With her moaning so loudly, I have no idea how much time we have left before Max or Cari break us up. Did they hear us? Do they care? River and I sure don't. We're making up for lost time.

"Fuck me, baby," I mutter, and she presses her pouty lips to my center.

River's tongue circles my clit before dipping inside me. She flattens her tongue and takes long, languid licks up and down. I grip her hair tightly, unable to move. I'm barely even able to stand up.

"Mmm," I mutter.

I play with my breasts, squeezing and tugging on my nipples. As much as I want to savor this moment, we're on borrowed time, and we both know it. I watch as River thrusts her tongue all around my pussy as she works overtime. Closing my eyes and attempting to be quiet, I drown out everything else. River sucks on my clit, and I'm a goner. My knuckles tighten around her hair, and I bite down on my bottom lip while I hold back my moans. I ride her face to my orgasm.

"Oh, fuck." River groans as she licks every last drop of me.

"Fuck," I mutter, letting go of her hair.

She stands, smiling with her messy sex hair and wet, swollen lips. She's the walking epitome of sex right now.

"Hey, uh are you almost done…*getting dressed?*" Cari says quietly, clearly not believing we were just getting changed in here.

"Yup! Just a minute!" River squeaks, her cheeks turning a bright tomato-red.

"Okay." We hear Cari's footsteps fade, and we both crack up.

"How much do you wanna bet Cari and Max did rock, paper, scissors to see who had to check on us?" I laugh.

"Oh, my gosh. They definitely heard." River hides her face in my chest.

"Yes, but at least you sounded good." I rub her hair but apparently that was the wrong thing to say because River playfully hits my shoulder.

"Get out of here. I have to get dressed now." She rolls her eyes.

"Fine." I place a kiss on her cheek, peek behind the curtain, and slide into the second changing area.

My clothes are neatly piled on the chair where I left them—minus the T-shirt I grabbed from the floor on my way out. I slide everything on. Then, I look in the mirror and attempt to fix my hair. It's all over the place, and my eyeliner is smudged. There will be no denying we just had sex.

River is still getting changed when I walk out, so I try to act casual…

Like I wasn't just tongue-deep in my ex-girlfriend.

Cari is staring at me, begging me to make eye contact with her, but I refuse. Walking over to where my makeup bag is, I grab what I need before packing everything up and pretending like everyone isn't staring at me.

Max walks over a few minutes later, and she has a big smile on her face.

"You have to see these." She's so happy; I guess the photos came out okay.

I follow her to the laptop that has all her photos uploading, and she starts showing me from the beginning. You can see the natural progression of River's nerves. I can almost pinpoint when I told her to focus on me and how she eased up. Max flips through a few more, and we get to the steamy session. Our kissing gets progressively more and more heated. To be honest, we look fucking hot.

I wouldn't want my mother seeing these, but the rest of the world? It's not anything I'm ashamed of. Even when we get to the photos of me with my shirt off, somehow Max has made it look classy. River's hands and mouth cover me in most of them, but there are a few where we forget we're being photographed. The look in River's eyes is anything but friendship. I just can't tell if it's lust or more.

"I might have to make this a series if this is as popular as I imagine it'll be. You two have amazing chemistry." Max smiles. "But you probably know that already." She winks.

I grimace. So they *did* hear us.

"Does that mean—"

"For the sake of our friendship, let's not talk about it." Max laughs.

"Okay." I nod. That's probably for the best.

River emerges from the dressing room in a jean miniskirt and a purple crop top. She's holding the lingerie and the boxers I left behind in a folded pile. Well, there was our last bit of discrepancy. I guess I should've remembered my boxers.

She hands the clothes to an assistant, and then Cari reaches her before I can. I don't know what they're talking about, but River is blushing and avoiding eye contact with me again. She's so cute when she gets embarrassed. I know what I saw and felt; if anything, knowing that people were listening only fueled her. If I didn't know better, I'd say she has a bit of a voyeurism kink.

"So, I know we had plans, but Cari invited me out to eat after this..." Max begins.

"No worries, have fun with her." I smile.

"Actually, it's with her *and* River. So maybe you want to come?" Max asks like she isn't sure. To be honest, I'm not sure either. I still have no idea where I stand with River.

"If I'm welcome, sure." I nod.

"I'll find out." Max walks over to Cari and River so I grab my things and pretend to be looking at my phone. I don't have any messages, so I just scroll Instagram for a few minutes.

"River might've turned bright-red when I said your name, but she also smiled when I asked if you could come to lunch." Max laughs.

"Cool," I say nonchalantly.

Max grabs her camera and says goodbye to her assistants, giving them the rest of her stuff to take back to her studio. Cari and River meet us out front, River's hair blowing in the breeze. I catch her laughing about something that Cari said, and I take a second to appreciate how relaxed she is. She's calm and herself again—back in her own clothes and with her best friend.

"Where we headed?" I ask reaching them.

"There's this cute lunch place about two blocks away. And I have an in, so we'll probably get free appetizers or something." Cari smiles.

"Nice." I nod.

Max and Cari walk ahead of us because the sidewalk is narrow. River and I are both quiet again. It seems to be a pattern with us: have sex and then run out of things to say to each other. I think it's just our way of learning how to be around each other again. When an old lady and a yippie chihuahua come blazing past us, River bumps into me and I catch my hand on her side to balance her.

"I'm sorry. I just hate chihuahuas." She sighs.

"Remember that time in high school when Michelle wanted one so bad ,so she adopted one from the pet store without telling her parents, and then it ate part of your homecoming dress?" I laugh.

"Yes! She wanted me to keep it at my house until she told them. But then I came home to her eating the dress after she peed in my shoes. Her parents made her give it back after that."

"Rightfully so."

"I don't know why anyone would want one of them."

"Me; they're like rat dogs. And in the city, just adopt a real rat at that point."

"Are you guys talking about adopting rats?" Cari raises an eyebrow, turning around.

"Yes, we were thinking about getting one and naming it after you," I joke.

"Funny." Cari scoffs.

"Aspen!" River shakes her head, laughing at me.

I don't get a chance to reply because Max is holding open the door to the restaurant. We file in while Cari speaks to the hostess. A minute later, we're being escorted to a private table on the second floor of the place. It isn't a fancy place by any means, but it's a nice place. There's pretty aesthetic art on the walls, and the tables are clearly new. The menu is extensive, but I find something I like, and Cari orders a few rounds of appetizers for us to share. She's right about getting something for free. It must be nice—just having to take a few photos and getting free food and products. Especially as a job.

"So, what's everyone getting?" Max asks, closing her menu.

"I'm getting the buffalo chicken egg rolls and a side of fries," I say.

"Ooh, can I steal some? That sounds so good, but I want to try the Mac and cheese bites with aioli sauce." River groans.

"Only if I can have some of yours."

"Deal." She nods eagerly.

"I'm having a Mexican steak bowl," Max says.

"I'm getting that too! It's so good from here." Cari smiles.

The waiter takes our order and brings us each a drink. Cari and Max splurge for a cocktail while River sticks to water. I get an iced tea and pop the straw in while they talk about some new show I haven't seen yet.

"Do you remember that time we snuck in to see the new Fifty Shades of Grey movie and then got kicked out?" River asks me.

"Yes, only because *someone* was hollering every time Dakota Johnson had her tits out," I tease.

"Hey, they're nice tits." She shrugs.

"They are." Max and Cari agree.

"Okay, true. But not at the time when we're underage to seeing the movie."

"We were barely underage; I think we were both what? Fifteen? Sixteen?"

"That's underage, I think it's rated R."

"For nudity! I've seen tits, I have tits, why can't I watch them on screen?" River says, her argument from a decade ago still ringing true.

"How did this come up anyway?"

"Dakota Johnson is in a new movie, this time with her tits concealed," River says, frowning.

"Ah," I chuckle.

River smiles at me, and my stomach flips. I feel like I can melt right into the seat I'm sitting in. She has that effect on me.

"So, Aspen, are you a full-time makeup artist?" Cari asks after our food arrives.

"Yeah, mostly freelance but every so often Max hooks me up with a job. Speaking of which, the bride whose makeup I did yesterday had a fashion designer friend, so I gave her your card."

"Wait, a pink-haired woman?"

"Yeah…"

"She messaged me this morning, but I had no idea who she's. I'll have to message her back. Thanks." Max smiles.

"Of course, she made the bride's dress and it's stunning. She's also queer."

"Perfect." Max is always down to expand our little circle.

River's hand rests on my thigh, and I bite the inside of my cheek. Is she making a move on me?

13. Strangers

RIVER

I place my hand on Aspen's thigh out of some subconscious habit. I don't mean to, but once it's there neither Aspen nor I move it. We eat and talk to our friends like there's not a million thoughts racing through my mind about today. I'm still aching for Aspen to touch me again. For her to put her hands, lips, anything on my body. So when Aspen finally puts her hand on my thigh, I smile. Her warm hand squeezes my right thigh lightly and lingers for a moment. Cari and Max excuse themselves to meet the owner. Something about Max wanting to shoot something here and Cari making the introduction.

"You're killing me in this skirt." Aspen growls when we're alone.

I turn to face her, and she smirks.

"Sorry." I shrug playfully.

"Maybe I should do something about it." Her green eyes darken with desire, and I freeze.

"What do you mean?" I ask.

Instead of answering, Aspen moves her hand up my thigh slowly. I feel like a teenager when you played that game with your friends, and you were supposed to tell them to stop before they got too close. But I don't stop Aspen. She looks at me, waiting for me to stop her or to say something. I don't. Her fingers reach the front of my panties, and I gasp.

"Tell me to stop. Tell me you don't want me to finger fuck you right now." Aspen leans in to whisper in my ear.

Our friends are only across the room talking with an older woman. But the booth is large, and you can't see anything going on below our shoulders. So I don't tell Aspen to stop. Instead, I look back at her and spread my thighs for her to give her easier access.

"Fuck," she mutters under her breath.

I pick up my glass of water and drink a sip, gripping it tightly as she slides my panties to the side and exposes my pussy to the air. I'm still wet from earlier, there's no denying that. I'm sure with all we did, I'll be wet for days.

Aspen trails a finger up my wet center, and I bite my cheek. I need to keep my cool if I want her to continue.

"That's it, spread your legs for me. But don't make a sound, or I have to stop," she warns.

She slides a finger in my core, and I clench my jaw. She moves it ever so slowly, then begins pumping. Aspen curls her finger and hits my G-spot perfectly. I keep one eye on our friends, even though it takes everything in me to do so. I just want to kiss Aspen and put my hands all over her again.

"Come on, baby. I know how badly you want to make a sound. We can't be silent, though. It has to look like we're at least talking," Aspen points out with a smirk.

"Add another," I mumble. I don't care what it looks like; I'm fucking soaked from earlier, and being touched by Aspen brings out an animalistic need in me.

"There's my girl, asking for what she wants." Aspen smirks. She licks her lips, moist and plump and just begging to be kissed. But I stay still.

"You need to make me come before they finish."

"Make you finish first, got it." Aspen winks.

"Aspen," I grumble just as she adds a second finger. With her spare hand, she picks up her drink and takes a lengthy sip while her other hand is working magic between my thighs. Fuck me.

"Uh oh, they're on their way back. Better hurry up, Riv." She winks and I move my hips. I'm going to ride her fucking hand to get my goddamn release. I have about thirty seconds, and I don't care. I grind my hips on her hand and look into her hazel eyes. Something about looking right at her sends me over the edge. Aspen praises me, but I can't hear her, I'm too busy wiggling on her hand desperate for a release. I'm dripping all over her hand, and I don't care. I need this. I need *her*. I fall into her shoulder, inhaling her sweet scent and muffling my moans. She slowly slides her hand out of me, and I assume she cleans it off with the napkin. I'm afraid to look at my friends. What we'd just done must be obvious. I decide to face the music, only to pull away from Aspen and see Max and Cari are still across the restaurant.

"I thought you said they were coming," I grumble at Aspen.

"Hey, you told me to make you come first." Aspen laughs.

"Ugh, that is so never happening again," I lie. I know it's a lie when the words slip out of my mouth.

"Okay." Aspen just shrugs.

"Thanks for introducing me. The owner is so nice." Max smiles at Cari as they reach the table. They sit back down across from us, completely unaware of what just went down.

"No problem. You guys ready to go? Bill is all taken care of." Cari looks between Aspen and me.

"I think we were gonna go for a walk, right Riv?" Aspen asks, smiling at me.

"A walk? Yes, sounds good." I nod.

"Okay." Cari furrows her brow at me, which I know means she'll be looking for an explanation later.

"Why don't I walk you home?" Max asks Cari.

"Sure." Cari nods. "See you guys later." She grabs her purse and Max shuffles her out the door.

"Fuck, you're so hot when you come." Aspen smirks.

"I can't believe we just did that," I say, breathless.

"Any regrets?"

"None whatsoever," I admit. That was hot as fuck, I just didn't expect to be so into it.

"We should get out of here before I think about doing it again," Aspen teases.

"Mhm." I stand, fixing my skirt, and then I follow Aspen outside.

"Why don't I walk you home? You can't be far from here, right?"

"Just a few blocks," I say looking up at the street sign. "But I have work soon."

"How about I walk you to work?"

"Sure." I nod. I don't know how I feel about this, or the thought of her meeting my co-workers, but I guess I would find out.

"I'm glad today worked out for Max. I would've felt so bad if she had to cancel her space," Aspen says.

"Me too. I was surprised to see you there today."

"I was surprised to see you, too. Max didn't mention it. But I have a feeling that might be with some help from Cari."

"That doesn't surprise me." I sigh. My best friend has a habit of meddling.

"At least it all worked out for the best."

We stop at the crosswalk, glancing in each direction and ignoring the light to cross anyway. It's New York City, no one gives a shit about traffic lights. We end up getting honked at by a yellow cab driver speeding around the corner. Aspen grabs my hand as we race across the street, laughing as we almost get sideswiped. It's just a hazard of the risk we took. Aspen doesn't let go of my hand when we cross the street, our hands interlocked. I think about saying something, but for whatever reason, I don't.

"What do you say the next time we run into each other, it's on purpose?" Aspen asks.

"Like you want to hang out again?" Is she asking me on a date or to hookup?

"Yeah, I mean if not, I understand..."

"No, we can. Maybe we should exchange numbers then?" I suggest.

"Sure." Aspen nods, so we stop at the corner before the shop and exchange numbers. It feels weird having Aspen's number in my phone again. I deleted it forever ago because it held too much power over me when I was drunk. It's safer that I didn't have access to it when my inhibitions were cloudy.

"My shop is just up the block," I point to the building, and Aspen looks at me.

"Can I see it? Or is that weird?" she asks rubbing the back of her head.

"No, you can. I don't know who's working today but my co-workers are my co-owners. We all split everything when it comes to this place."

"That's awesome. It'll be cool to see what you've done for yourself in the last few years," Aspen says. Her words leave a bitter taste on my tongue. She wouldn't have to be seeing it for the first time if she had never left. But right now isn't the time to open that can of worms.

I just nod and lead her up to the shop. The elevator ride is quiet; I'm not sure what to say to fill the silence. And I guess she doesn't know either. When we step inside, the shop is empty except for Gus's music playing loudly—which means they're the only one here.

"Gus? It's River! I'm here a little early!" I say, looking at the clock above the front desk.

"River! Hey!" Gus pops their head out of their room and lowers the music.

"Hey, this is Aspen. I was just showing her around," I explain. Gus shoots me a quick look and then smiles at Aspen.

"Nice to meet you." They shake hands awkwardly.

"I'm guessing Rae and Isla aren't here yet, then?"

"Nah, they don't have appointments until three p.m., so they said they'll be late." Gus shrugs.

"Why don't I show you my office of sorts." I lead Aspen down the hall and show her my room. I left it in pristine condition, thankfully.

"Shit, this is a nice ass place," Aspen saying looking around the room. "Did you do these?" She points at the art pieces framed on the walls.

"Yeah, some I've actually tattooed on people and some I just made." I shrug.

"These are *really* good."

"You sound surprised," I tease.

"Not at all. I'm just impressed. I haven't seen your art in forever. I didn't know what route you'd go with it, but tattooing it on people is amazing." She smiles.

"Thanks, it's a very relaxing and fun job for me. It makes me not feel like I'm not working," I admit.

"Do you get along with everyone?"

"Oh yeah, they're like my second family."

"I wish I had that; I mean, I do with Max and her roommates. But like in my job, everything is so lonely. I work by myself and go to clients alone. I don't have anyone in my life that does what I do. Not that I spend a lot of time with, anyway."

"I understand that. It's better with people. When I was freelancing at random shops until we opened this one, I hated it. I loved the job itself, but there was no stability and no sense of family," I say.

"It's kind of like that with being a makeup artist. That's why I like collaborating with Max when I can. Or even other photographers," Aspen explains.

"Hey, River. You have a walk in," Gus says poking their head in the room.

"Sure, give me a minute," I say before turning to face Aspen.

"So, I'll text you? Maybe we can plan something a little less impromptu?" Aspen asks.

"I'd like that." I nod. I know I'm playing with fire. I mean, sex is one thing but whatever is going on between Aspen and I feels like more than that. Feels like more than I can even properly explain.

"Have a good day at work." She leans in, and I think she's about to kiss me but instead she turns her head slightly. She presses her lips gently to my cheek and then heads out the door.

My cheek burns where her lips just were.

14. Lead Me On

ASPEN

"Did you buy me the vodka I was looking for?" my mother asks the moment I walk in the house.

"No. The store was closed," I lie. She knows it's a lie too. That's why she scoffs and sits back down on the couch.

I refuse to be part of her bad habit. But no matter how many times I've told her that, she doesn't seem to care. To her, I'm just a means to getting what she wants. If I'm not willing to help her, she doesn't care enough to even talk to me. It's been like this for longer than I care to admit, but it's gotten worse since she got her diagnosis. If anything, she should be trying to get sober so she can get on the transplant list and have a chance at life. I mean, people survive liver cancer. My mother seems determined not to be on the favorable end of that statistic.

"If you can't help me out then why are you even here?" she grumbles, pulling a beer out of her small cooler from next to the couch. I should've known she'd have a backup option. I think one of the neighbors is buying them, but I can't be too sure of who.

"I'm here to take care of you; that's what dad would've wanted," I point out. She freezes at my mention of him.

She doesn't say anything. Usually, when I mention him, it's the last she'll speak for the night. Maybe that's why I brought him up to begin with.

I clear the empty bottles from around her on the table and head toward the kitchen. She clearly cooked something in my absence, but I can't tell what it was. I'm supposed to be making sure she eats and takes care of herself, but it's clear she plans on drinking herself into early grave.

I know my dad must be watching down at us and just thinking about how disappointed he is. All I've ever wanted to do is make him proud, and I can barely keep mom sober enough to not pee herself or walk outside before putting pants on. I'm doing my best, but I can't do everything. I sigh as I clean up after her.

I start a fresh load of laundry and try to think about literally anything or anyone else. Of course, River pops into my head. The vision of sixteen-year-old River sitting on the washing machine rushes back to me. It was one of the only places we could be alone back then. We'd sneak down here to "do laundry" and make-out on said washing machine. We'd both had many orgasms on the high setting.

I texted her earlier, after leaving her at work, but I haven't heard back yet. I'm not sure when I will, but I hope I do. I know things are different between us now, but one thing is certain—I want River in my life…in any way she'll have me. If it's just sex or as just her friend, I can accept it. Well, I'll force myself to accept it.

I knew it's stupid. I'm clearly still in love with River; there is no denying that. But with her being so hot and cold, I'm not sure where we stand. We obviously still have the same chemistry we used to, but beyond that, I don't know what's happening. Chemistry can only get us so far. I want something real, but does she? Or are we both just reliving some teenage fantasy of being with our first loves again?

My thoughts are interrupted by the sound of my mother throwing a beer bottle. It's a sound I know all too well from my childhood here. I can tell by the sound that she hit the wall right next to the television. So something on the news must've pissed her off.

Not that I can blame her; the news is a dumpster fire these days. I have no idea why she insists on watching it. Thankfully, I've only been on the end of her abuse emotionally and not physically. I wasn't always as tall as I am now. She could've easily overpowered me when I was younger.

I sit down against the washing machine and shake my head. I'm trapped in here now, unless I want to see the aftermath of one of her rampages. She's only gotten worse since her diagnosis. I'm not sure if she even remembers she's sick most days. I can't tell what's a symptom of her cancer and what's from her excessive drinking at this point.

I stretch my legs out on the cool marble floor of the unfinished basement and frown. If I could, I would pack up and head back to California. But I know how much it took for her to call me six months ago. When she told me she's sick and that she needed me to come home? That took all of the pride she had left, and I know it. I'm the only one left. My dad got into a car accident when I was twelve and died instantly. I think the other driver is still in jail, but honestly, I don't even care to think about them. My dad is gone and that's the only thing that matters.

I don't know where the tears come from, but they start running down my cheeks as if each one is in a race with the last. I know I deserve better than this, but I don't know what to do. I mean, she's my *mom*. How could I not take care of her?

I close my eyes and think about River again. My phone buzzes in my pocket, and I reach for it, hoping it's from her. Surprisingly, it is. A short *hey*, replying to my hello.

It's like we're starting at the beginning all over again. We're fifteen again, learning about each other. We've changed so much in the last five years, but at our cores, we're still us.

ME:

Are you still at work?

RIVER:

Yup, working late tonight with Gus. HBY?

ME:

Just doing laundry, catching up on chores.

RIVER:

Ugh, can you do mine? I'm so behind it's not even funny.

ME:

Sure, just send it over lol.

RIVER:

Don't tempt me with a good time. I hate doing laundry so much, I've sent out for it to be done way too many times. Or just bought fresh panties.

ME:

Why buy new panties when you could just go commando?

RIVER:

I get too wet for that 😏

ME:

Oh, I know...

RIVER:

BRB client.

I put my phone back in my pocket and wait for another lull in River's day. I know it's a problem that talking to her is easily the best part of my night. Touching her was the best part of my day. I could replay the photo shoot in my mind all damn day. Her body on mine, the way we fell into each other naturally, and how fucking good she felt. Fuck. The thought of other people seeing those photos is enough to make me jealous.

I did my best to cover her up as much as possible. Sure, she thought it was for her. But in reality? I didn't want anyone seeing River in the ways I did. I wanted to keep her to myself as much as possible. I don't like to share, and I don't even want our friends knowing how lucky I have it. Then again, maybe fucking in the changing room beside them wasn't the best move. But I couldn't keep my hands off of her. She's gorgeous and my hands are like magnets to her body.

I wait until the laundry beeps so I can switch it to the dryer, and I hear silence from above. My mother is probably fast asleep on the couch by now, so I can make my way upstairs. There's no need for sneaking around.

I head upstairs and grab a water from the fridge and a protein bar from my drawer, and then I go upstairs. I glance at my mom on the way up and see she's passed out on the armchair just like I assumed. I'm too tired to attempt to throw out the rest of her beer. Besides, she's a grown up. If she wants to drink herself to death, why should I try to stop her?

I know why I should. She's my *mom*. But isn't she supposed to be the one taking care of me?

RIVER:
You up?

ME:
Is this a booty call?

RIVER:
U wish 😂 I just got out of work.

ME:
I do wish. Say the time & place. 😏

RIVER:
How'd the laundry go? You should've cleaned your mind since it's so dirty 😜

ME:
Never had any complaints before.

RIVER:
Show me the written complaint form please.

> **ME:**
> Ouch.

> **RIVER:**
> Work was so lame today. Someone wanted a dreamcatcher on their thigh 😭 what is this, 2009?!

> **ME:**
> Well there goes my next tattoo idea.

> **RIVER:**
> Oh, shut it. I love tattooing but I live for the days when it's something more creative, that's all.

> **ME:**
> What's the coolest thing you've tatted? Or is that like doctors with HIPPA? You can't talk about it?

> **RIVER:**
> Nah, it's a full back piece of quotes from this author that their partner wrote. It's sick.

> **ME:**
> Pics??

> **RIVER:**
> Excuse me?

> **ME:**
> Of the tattoo LMAO!

> **RIVER:**
> Oh. I'd have to scroll insta for a while. It was a few years ago.

> **ME:**
> Gotcha.

River and I go back and forth while I fold the laundry. When it's all done and put away, I lounge in my bed and consider turning my TV on. But in reality, it would only be background noise to my texts with

River. She's my focus tonight. We're talking about everything and somehow nothing at all. We have a million things to say to each other, and the conversation flows naturally. We've texted for about an hour when my phone lights up with a phone call from her.

"Hello?"

"My hands are hurting, so I need to use my hand massager. I figured I'd just call you," she explains.

"Hand massager?" I smirk.

"There's that dirty mind again. It really is a hand massager. I have to keep my babies in tip-top shape."

"Makes sense."

"What are you up to now?"

"Just lying in bed."

"What are you wearing?" she asks in a sultry voice.

"Are you serious?" I sit up in bed, waiting for her answer.

Laughter fills the room. "No! I'm sorry, I just can't. I'm just messing around. Don't get so excited."

"I was just shocked. I didn't think you'd be the one initiating phone sex." I laugh.

"Maybe not tonight." She laughs. I don't push further. She's implying we might have the chance to talk again, and it makes my heart swell.

"So when can I see you again?"

"I don't know, when are you free?"

"Whenever you are."

"I'm serious, Aspen."

"I have work tomorrow, but I'm free the day after," I say, glancing at my calendar.

"That works for me. I have a morning session, but I'm free after that. What do you want to do?"

"You mean besides you?"

"Oh, my gosh!"

"I was thinking we could go out to a real meal and try to keep our clothes on. If you can handle that," I tease.

"I think I can manage if you keep your hands to yourself."

"No promises."

"Why am I not surprised?"

"If you really want me to, I'll be a perfect gentlewoman," I promise.

"Well, maybe don't go that far…"

"Oh, Riv. You're a girl after my own panties."

15. Over My Head

RIVER

It's after four in the morning when Aspen and I finally hang up. I don't remember the last time I was on the phone with someone this long and didn't run out of things to talk about. We would've kept talking, but she has work tomorrow—well, today. We said our goodbyes, but all I want to do is keep talking to her. I hate that I'm letting her in like this again. I'm too weak to admit what might happen to me if I let her in again.

Since I'm wide awake, I decide to go looking for something. I know it's in the back of my closet somewhere, I'm just not entirely sure where. I've moved a few times, and it's probably something I should've gotten rid of, but I don't know how. Each time I look at it, I take a few mementos out. I figure at some point, I'll get over her and just toss out the whole box. I never expected her to come back into my life.

I move the boxes of art supplies I never use and find it on the top shelf just out of my reach. I grab a chair from the kitchen, trying not to make too much noise since it is four a.m. I grab the black box and look at all the photos it's covered in—all of the two of us...Aspen and me. She gave it to me for our first anniversary, and I kept it as a memory box of our relationship. I didn't have the heart to get rid of it when we broke up, despite how badly it hurt when she left.

I open the box, bracing myself for what's inside. I haven't looked at it in a while. I usually only look at it when I'm drunk and alone and crying about my future and being single. I thankfully haven't had one of those moments since I started seeing my therapist a few years back. She'd probably say this is a backtracking moment, but I don't think she has a romantic bone in her body. I mean, sometimes things aren't just black-and-white.

I pull out the letters she sent me. The ones covered in her lipstick-stained kisses, the photos of us at high school graduation, Pride, date nights over the years. There are more photo booth photos than I can count. Each one documents a different place we had been. But it's the little Lego people that I had custom made to look like us that stops me.

She's a fan of Legos. I could always find her putting them together back in the day. So, I had found pieces that looked exactly like us and painted on our names onto their shirts. But then Aspen broke up with me, and I never was able to show her. It's just one of the many things that halted my life. Aspen breaking up with me was out of the blue.

Sure, we were a normal couple who fought. But there was never any malice between us. We were about to graduate from college and move in together. We were only twenty-two, and it felt like we had the whole world ahead of us. We would be able to do everything together. I was one of the lucky ones who found the love of my life so young. Then, it was like the rug was snatched out from under me and I was blinded by Aspen.

"I don't think I can do this anymore."

"I'm not ready to be tied down."

"I think we should live our lives apart."

It hit me so hard. She was my first love. Hearing her say she wasn't ready to be with me and that she was feeling *tied down* broke me. It still hurts to think about it. I sigh, looking through everything, and I start to feel the tears fall. I didn't even realize I was holding them back until they break free. I wipe them with the back of my hand and slump onto the floor in my closet.

It's been five years, and it's like the tears are brand-new. It's like everything is fresh and raw. Like someone ripped out my heart and is plunging a needle in and out of it all over again. I know everyone always assumed Aspen and I wouldn't last, I mean she was my first love. But at the time, I hadn't thought that at all. Maybe it was puppy love or maybe it was me being naive. But the day Aspen told me she didn't want to be with me was one of the worst days of my life. It still hurts now, and I have her back in my life again.

Am I stupid for thinking about restarting things with Aspen again? I know I keep pushing it out of my mind, but that's where things are headed. She had asked me out, and we're talking at all hours of the night. Oh, and all the mind-blowing sex. Am I setting myself up for disaster? How am I supposed to know if Aspen still feels the same. How am I to know she won't get my hopes up only to dash them and leave all over again?

I guess I don't.

Is that a risk I'm willing to take? Am I really going to let her in again and possibly go through all that heartache? Is she worth the pain?

As much as I'm not totally sure, I also know I'm not the same person I was when I was twenty-two. And thank fuck for that. I was young and naive. I thought if Aspen and I were together, we could accomplish anything. I know that's not true now. I know how much I've grown up and into someone else. Could I say the same for Aspen? It's been almost five years, and she's a successful makeup artist. She has a group of awesome friends, and she's living with her mom. That last one gives me pause, because I know there must be a deeper story there. Things have changed with her; her life is different than I last saw it, so of course things are different.

I pause. I rub the tattoo of the ladybug behind my ear. It's subconscious, I'd always touch it when I thought about Aspen. Because it's the only tattoo I had that represented someone else. That represented *her*. Of course she didn't know about it, but it's another thing I had gotten just before we ended things. Before she broke up with me. The first time she told me she loved me, a ladybug appeared on her cheek. She almost freaked out, thinking it's a gross bug. But instead, I caught it and she just smiled and told me she loved me. It's simple and I knew she hadn't planned it out. I said those words back to her and from then on, I was obsessed with ladybugs. It's something I kept mostly to myself.

I wish someone would tell me how to feel about all of this.

I know just the person.

"Hello?" Cari answers on the first ring. She's my best friend and the only one who will be upfront with me about everything.

"I need you to be honest with me—"

"Is this about Aspen? I've been waiting for this call."

"Yes." I sigh. Of course, Cari knew, she knew me better than anyone.

"You're considering getting back together with her huh?"

"Yeah. I mean I don't even know if that's something she wants—"

"What about what you want?"

"What?"

"Well, you're saying you don't know what she wants. But what about you? I saw her absolutely *break* you, babe. I'm not saying you shouldn't go for this, but you need to be ready to take whatever answer she gives you."

"You think she'll say no?"

"Now that I didn't say."

"Cari..." I grumble.

"What do you want? From her?"

"I—I think I want to be with her. Romantically. Like we used to be but more seriously since we're older," I admit. It's the first time I've truly admitted it to myself, let alone out loud.

"Okay. Now have you thought about telling her that?"

"No, are you crazy?" I've never been the tell someone my deepest, darkest feelings type. It's why I've barely dated these last few years.

"You're the crazy one if you think she doesn't still have feelings for you. That woman is head over heels in love with you, and I can't believe you don't see it." Cari scoffs.

"She is?" I whisper.

"She is. If she's what you want, I can tell you she still loves you. But as far as a commitment, you know she's never the best at that. So I can't promise anything."

"Okay."

"What are you going to do?"

"I don't know," I admit, still unsure.

"Take some time, babe. Maybe no more hooking up in the meantime? Especially in random dressing rooms…"

"Oh my gosh." My cheeks burn, and I'm glad she can't see me right now.

"Hey, it's hot. But it might be confusing if you keep adding sex with your ex to the equation."

"You're right." I nod. I hate it, but she's right.

"Oh, Max wants me to tell you that she's gonna email you the photos from the shoot."

My heart stops. *Cari is with Max right now?*

"Uhh…"

"I can hear your panic. Max is in the other room. I'm on my balcony. So all of NYC could hear me, but not her. She just popped out to hand me a drink and I mouthed who I was on the phone with. Your secrets are safe with me, as always." Cari calms me down off the ledge. I don't want Aspen's best friend knowing how I feel before I even fully decide how I feel.

"Phew." I nod. "I'll let you get back then."

"Okay, but if you need me, text me. I'll try to answer between sex, but she likes to go at it for hours."

"Okay, hanging up now." I shake my head. My best friend loves sharing details. Too many details.

I look back at the pile of things from Aspen, and I feel calm. Maybe I'm stupid for thinking about it, but how could I not at least consider her? How could I not at least consider the fact that she's changed. That maybe now we're on the same page and we want the same things? Maybe all I need to do is have a conversation with her instead of hiding out in our memories. As much as I want to remember the old Aspen, maybe it's a good thing to leave all of this in the past. Maybe instead of staring into the past, I should be focusing on who she is now and what we could have.

16. Lover

ASPEN

River asks me to meet her at her apartment instead of at the restaurant, and I can't tell if that's a good thing or not. My palms are sweaty by the time I reach her building, and I try to get myself to calm down. I didn't think I was that nervous until I was here. I mean, it must be a good thing that she at least wants to see me, right? She technically can't even breakup with me since we aren't even dating. Somehow that thought isn't as comforting as I expected it to be.

Her doorman lets me in, and I head for the elevator. Pressing the button for her floor, I relax a bit. Whatever it is, we'll figure it out. Maybe this is the *talk*. Maybe she wants to talk about what the hell we've been doing and what we both want. That's even less comforting. What if we don't want the same thing? Will she even give me another chance after the way I left her last time? I don't blame her if she doesn't. I was young and dumb. There's no other way to explain it.

I knock on her door and brace myself for whatever is to come.

"Hey." River smiles as she opens the door.

I walk in and put my shoes next to hers. Am I supposed to kiss her? We haven't done a kiss greeting yet, but it's weird to just say hello.

"Hi," I say lamely. I'm overthinking things for sure.

"So, I was thinking maybe we could talk…" River's voice trails off as she walks into the living room and sits on her couch cross-legged.

"Sure." I nod. So, I was right.

"It just doesn't make sense for us to continue without talking about this. We're both grown-ups, and it's silly to pretend like whatever this is isn't happening," she explains.

"That's true." I tread lightly. This doesn't sound like a breakup conversation.

"So, I think that I might have feelings for you…again." She visibly swallows. Okay, definitely not a breakup conversation.

"I, uh, definitely have feelings for you again, too." I take a seat across from her on the couch. Leaning on one knee, I look at River and wait for her to say something. It feels like I could cut the tension with a knife. I have no clue where this conversation is headed.

"I just don't know where that leaves us," she says quietly.

"What do you mean?" I raise an eyebrow.

"I mean, we did this already. And you left because you couldn't handle the commitment. Which, granted, we were twenty-two. But I can't do this again if you're just going to leave."

"You're worried about me not wanting the same things?"

"Yes." She nods.

"Well, what are you looking for?" I ask.

"I mean I'm not like in a rush to get married or anything, but that is my intention of dating someone. I don't want to date someone I have no real future with. I'm twenty- seven and I'm over dating just to see where things go."

"That's understandable."

"What about you?"

I hesitate. I haven't given much thought to River and I getting back together and what I might want if she gives me the chance. My last few relationships have all been dumpster fires. Am I really in any place to start something with River? But, fuck. I look at her, and I can't imagine not being with her again. If this is my last chance to try something with her, then I have to go for it.

"I don't think I'm ready to get married right now, but I'd be lying if I said I didn't see that in my future if it was with you. I'm not looking to waste your time if that's what you're worried about."

"You're looking for a relationship, then?"

"Well, no. I'm not looking for one, I wasn't at least. But if you're saying the only thing you want is a relationship right now, then I'd be a fool to let you go twice," I admit.

"Really?"

"I was a fool to let you go five years ago, Riv. But I also think it was necessary. I was young and stupid, and I think it would've ruined us if I didn't have a chance to be on my own. I'm forever sorry that I hurt you, but I don't think we'd be who we are today if we didn't have a chance to grow apart."

"I was thinking that too. I don't know if I would've had the courage to open my own shop and stand on my own. We were so tied in each other it was hard to see beyond us," River says.

"I'd love another chance with you, Riv. I have feelings, and if you give me the chance to see where this can go, I promise not to break your heart again."

"Okay." She nods.

"Okay?" I raise a brow.

"Yeah, I think I'd like to see where this goes. I want you back. But you better not break my heart again," she warns in a fake menacing tone. She's about as scary as a rabbit, but I let her think I'm scared.

"Oh, I promise." I cross my heart with my fingers, and she laughs.

"Now get over here and kiss me," she commands.

"Yes ma'am." I nod.

I slide over to her side of the couch, take her face in my hands, and press my lips to hers. She purrs into my mouth, and fuck, I'm a goner. River wraps her legs around my waist as we both fall back to the couch. Her hands run across my body, sliding all over. I hold her tightly, my grip on her couch holding me from crushing her. Her tongue sweeps across mine, and I groan lightly into her mouth. I battle the urge to rip all her clothes off and take her on this couch.

If she's my girl now, I want to savor this. I want her to know how much she means to me. I'm still going to make her come so many times she loses count, but I also want to take her to dinner first. She kisses my neck, and I forget how to breathe; my eyes close as she nibbles lightly on the skin around the nape of my neck. She knows exactly what she's doing to me.

"Oh, fuck," I moan into her ear.

"Mmm," she hums against my skin.

She touches my breasts through my shirt, starting to unbutton the top ones when I catch her hands. She stares at me like a deer in headlights.

"As much as I want this, and god I want this, I want to at least take my new girlfriend out to dinner before I have her for dessert."

"No."

"No?" I look at her confused.

"How about we have dessert first?" She smirks.

"Riv," I groan. *How could I say no to something like that?* "How about I get you off, we go out, and then I eat you on your kitchen counter for dessert?"

"Yes please." She nods.

"Then lie down and undo those jeans for me, baby." I growl.

Her dark hair is tied in a ponytail today, containing her luscious curls, and all I want to do is pull it. I'll save that for later, though. Instead, I wrap one hand around her throat and bend down to kiss her. She's grinding her hips on mine, and I know she must be more turned-on than she's letting on. She's not normally so forward. I slide a hand between us and down the center to feel a wet spot on her panties. River's pussy is dripping for me. I have to bite back a groan. I rub her clit lightly through her panties and watch her squirm under me. God, I love teasing her. But this is a quickie, so I slip my fingers inside her panties and into her folds.

"Oh!" she cries out as I make contact with her bare skin.

My fingers slide around in her wetness, covering them

completely before I slip them inside her and curl them. My two fingers pump in and out as River moans under me.

"Oh, Aspen," she cries out my name, and it's music to my ears.

"That's right baby, I wanna make you come. Because you're all mine. Say you're all mine."

"I'm all yours." She whimpers.

I press my thumb to her clit, and she bucks her hips into mine. I bend down to kiss her, gliding my lips over hers and sliding my tongue into her mouth. She sucks lightly on my tongue, and I moan. Her hands reach for my breasts, and I flick my thumb against her clit again and again. River starts to shake, and I know she's about to come for me.

"Come for me, baby. Say my name," I command in her ear.

"Oh, ASPEN!" River *screams* for me. There is nothing sexier than watching a woman come undone.

"Mmm, that's my girl," I praise. I gently remove my fingers and lick them clean before sliding next to her on the couch. River's eyes are closed—a sign she's in orgasm heaven.

"I don't think I can move," she mumbles.

"Give it time; the feeling in your legs will come back." I laugh.

"I hope so." She laughs, too.

She peeks open her eyes and kisses me softly on the lips. I run my hand down her arm, tracing the outline of her tattoos. I still don't know how many she has or what each one is. Do they all have a story or are they just things River likes? I have so much to learn about her again, and I can't wait.

"Come on, we gotta go before it's too late to get a table," I say, sitting up.

"We live in New York City; it's never too late to get a table," she says sassily.

"Okay true, but I'm hungry." She doesn't move. "The quicker we go out, the quicker *I* get to eat."

"Oh." River's eyes light up and she sits up next to me. "Fine, but I have to go change my panties."

"Sure, I'll be here." I nod.

"You're not coming with me?" She bats her eyelashes.

"Nope, you and no panties in a room with a bed? I'm not falling for that," I tease.

"Ah you're no fun." She laughs.

Five minutes later, she's in a new pair of panties and her hair is touched-up. She's done just enough to cover up the fact that we just had sex. I had called a place nearby and got a reservation while she was getting ready, so I tell her how to get there, and we take off. I'm pretty freaking turned-on, but I'm determined to ignore it and take her out on an actual date. Besides, later we'll have all night to do whatever I want with her.

I make a mental note to pick up some whipped cream on the way home.

We walk out of the building, and I grab River's hand. Not for any other reason than because I want to. And because I can. She's mine again, and I'm going to do everything in my power to keep it that way. She deserves to be treated like the princess she is. I glance at her and smile. She's not looking my way, but damn. I feel like I'm sixteen all over again. River is mine and all is right in the world. I just need to make sure it stays that way.

17. Antidote

ASPEN

"Are you ready for tonight?" I ask River as I sit on her bed, waiting for her to get dressed.

I got ready at my place, opting for a black jumpsuit with a sparkly long-sleeved top. My heels are at least five inches and my feet will be killing me tomorrow, but I don't care. I look hot.

The anticipation of seeing River is killing me. She got dressed in her closet, so I can't see what's under her clothes.

When she comes out, I tell her it makes no sense since I'll be the one undressing her later. She gives me a line about building up anticipation, but her tits are out so I'm not really listening.

"Can you zip me up?" River walks out backward in a reddish-orange dress that clings to her body.

"Mmm." I clear my throat and zip her dress, stopping to kiss her bare shoulders.

"How do I look?" She spins around and my jaw drops. Every time I see her all made-up like this it makes my heart—and my panties—melt.

Her dress is classy, but it shows off just enough cleavage to tease me. Her thin straps hold up the dress that goes down to her calves. Her tattooed arms look like real art with small glimpses of her other pieces on display as well. A large slit travels up her right leg, exposing a good portion of her thigh. She's wearing a pair of heels as tall as mine, and I'm in heaven.

"Fuck, you look sexy as hell." I smile.

"Yeah?" She fixes her dress and twirls her hair. It's natural today, her curls in full volume and exploding all over her shoulders and down her back.

"Are you nervous?" I ask, but I already know the answer.

"Maybe," she admits.

"It's just some people looking at photos of us; it'll be alright," I reassure her.

"But it's a *lot* of people looking at us with *not* a lot of clothes," she whispers.

"I know, but hey, at least I kept all the goods on you concealed. And Max already showed us which ones she chose for the gallery. So it's not really a surprise," I remind her.

"That's true." She nods. River lifts a silver necklace to her neck, and I hold up her hair so she can put it on without getting tangled.

"We should get going, though; Max said to make sure we aren't late."

"I think that was directed at you." She laughs.

"Touché."

I slip my phone in my back pocket and leave everything else on River's nightstand. I don't need anything else tonight. I'll be coming back here, and I have money and a metro card activated on my phone.

The gallery is only six blocks from River's apartment, so we decide to walk. The weather is surprisingly nice, and we don't mind the exercise. My feet will be killing me no matter what. Besides, it isn't worth it to take a fifty-dollar Uber ride.

Although we went out last week, this is our first *official* date, and I want to make sure everything goes smoothly. I have plans for us for after the gallery, too, but River doesn't know it yet. I take her hand in mine, linking our fingers together, and River smiles at me. I know she's nervous about tonight, but I'm honestly excited. I can feel my body radiating with excitement, each nerve doing a little dance. The photos are amazing, and they are part of why River is in my life again. I couldn't be more grateful to Max for bringing us back together.

When we arrive, Cari is pouring Max a glass of champagne and talking to people. We don't want to interrupt in case they're potential buyers, so we wave casually and then look around. The first wall has a few pieces by Max, but they aren't of River and me. They are of another couple she shot, and while they look good, they aren't us.

A waiter comes by with a tray of champagne, but River and I politely decline. I think she declines because of me. We haven't had the awkward talk about why I don't drink anymore, but I've been sober for six months, since my mother's diagnosis, and I can't imagine having it any other way. I don't want to risk turning into my mother. I can easily live without alcohol, but I don't want River to feel like she has to. If she wants to have a drink now and then, I'm not going to stand in her way. But telling River all this means telling her about my mom. And while I don't want to keep any secrets from her, I'm just not ready to open that can of worms yet. The topic of my mother is a mess, and I want to stay clean just a little while longer.

"I think our pieces are on the other side of this wall, because anyone who walks past it keeps looking at us," River whispers to me.

"Then let's go see." I squeeze her hand gently and guide her the way she's looking.

"Whoa!" River says and my jaw drops at the same moment.

There is definitely something different about seeing yourself in a gallery, on a wall, half-naked for the world to see. Something kind of intimidating while also … amazing? It's hard to explain. My eyes pull from the photo to make sure River is okay. If it's too much for her, I'll have her out of here and in a cab in minutes. Max would just have to understand. River isn't upset though. She looks just as amazed as I am.

The first piece is River and me on the bed, her hips grinding on me. Her hair is natural, flowing behind her, and she looks like a goddess. Her eyes are closed, but she looks euphoric. My face is out of the shot, but I remember that moment perfectly.

The second shot is us on the bed kissing; our hands are all over each other. It's extremely sensual and romantic. It's like we were saying more with our bodies than we could with our mouths. I blush. It's such an intimate moment for us to share with the world. Still, I'm also glad it was captured. If I weren't so poor, I'd buy the whole collection from Max myself.

The last photo might actually be my favorite. We were against the mirror, Max was nowhere in sight, and the photo is in black-and-white. River had her body against mine, her mouth against my bare breast, and my nipple in her mouth. I can still feel the sensations of how good it felt to be close to her.

"Holy shit, is that you guys?" A younger woman turns around and gapes at us. River tenses but I squeeze her hand gently to reassure her.

"Yeah." I nod.

"You both look amazing." The woman smiles, then turns to her partner and whispers something.

River leans into my chest, and I run my hand down her bare arm. She lets out a low sigh and we continue walking through the gallery. There's only a few more photos of us, but Max stops us before we have a chance to check them out.

"I'm so glad you both made it!" She hugs us both at once, which might be the third time Max and I have hugged in all our lives.

"It's such a great turnout, right?" Cari gushes by Max's side.

"Yeah, this one made a few posts about it." Max elbows Cari playfully.

"You both look amazing." River smiles.

"You're really the stars of the show tonight. Everyone is *obsessed* that the models who brought the steam are actually here tonight. I'm so glad you came!" Max grins at River and me.

"We can't take credit for that; your work definitely deserves to be here." River blushes.

"She got four offers to do another set of shots similar to yours,"

Cari says proudly. I still don't know what's going on with them relationship-wise, but things seem to be going well.

"Wow. That's incredible." I smile. That's no small feat for Max. It's about time they're finally getting admired for their talent.

"Max, can we get some photos of you with the models?" someone with a camera asks.

"Do you guys mind?" Max looks at us.

I look at River, who nods. "Nah."

Cari takes a step back, letting the photographer take a few photos of us, and I hold River close to me as we pose. I want the world to know they might be able to see her like this in a photo, but she's still mine.

"Perfect, thanks." The woman smiles and takes off to view the rest of the gallery.

"I should mingle, but thank you guys a million times over for everything." Max smiles at us both walks away with Cari.

River flutters to my side, looks at me, and surprises me by leaning in for a kiss. Her lips meet mine, and I melt into her. God, I love this woman. I knew it five years ago, but it's even more evident now. I couldn't imagine not being with her anymore. Her tongue slips in my mouth, and I forget where we are and that people can see us. In this moment, all I want is to feel as much of River as she's giving me. She pulls away slowly, leaving a peck on my lips. Her red lipstick is slightly smudged, so I use my thumb to slide it across her bottom lip to fix it.

"Get a room!" someone yells.

I blush and realize we've created a bit of a crowd. They probably assumed we're some sort of live installation in the gallery. I take River's hand and look at the small crowd.

"Okay, shows over!" I call out. The crowd disperses and River is a deep red, the same shade as her lipstick.

"Why don't we get out of here?"

"Sounds good." River says.

I lead her out the door, making a mental note to text Max later. I don't want to bother her again with a quick goodbye. She has more important people to talk to tonight, and I don't want to get in the middle of anything. Besides, there's somewhere I want to take River. And while the night is still young, too. I want to get there before our feet are too tired.

"Where are we going? My apartment is in the other direction," River asks, clearly confused as I lead her down the avenue.

"I thought maybe we'd go to *Scissors*," I say with a smile.

"Scissors?! Really?" Her face lights up just as I had hoped.

"I heard they're having a DJ tonight. We can go dancing for a bit," I explain.

"I would love that!" She claps and looks so excited.

"Then let's go."

I lead her down the street, and a few blocks later, we're outside the lesbian club: *Scissors*. We used to come here all the time when we dated the first time, so I thought it might be a cute way for us to take a trip down memory lane. We wait in line for the bouncer to let us in, pay an overpriced cover charge, and finally head inside.

It's almost the same as I remember it. There's dim lighting, the smell of cheap beer, and my heels stick to the floor. But the smile on River's face is *so* worth it. She looks up at me and smiles. She's standing before me at twenty-seven, but for just a second, she's sixteen and looking at me for the first time.

And in this moment, I'm even more in love with her than before.

18. Crush

RIVER

Aspen and I dance in the middle of the dance floor at *Scissors*. Our bodies grind while I toss my shoulders back and feel the vibration of the music through my heels. My feet are killing me, but I'm not letting up. It's been years since I've been here. I think last time was with Aspen. I forgot how much I enjoy just dancing with someone.

Aspen holds my waist steady as I move around her. She leans in for a steamy kiss, holding the back of my neck with one hand and sliding her tongue in my mouth. God, I love the way she kisses. It's like we were made for each other. I'm sober but drunk off the energy of the night. I can feel everything all at once, and it feels amazing.

"Are you having fun?!" Aspen leans in to yell in my ear.

"Yes!" I nod back.

I could barely hear her over the pounding music, but I don't want to go yet. Seeing myself on the walls of the gallery was invigorating. I had been so nervous about it, but then seeing them with Aspen by my side, I was sort of...turned-on. She looked so beautiful, and Max made us look like ourselves, keeping us natural but also making us look like a real models.

Then that *kiss*. I could kiss Aspen all night if she would let me. I want to kiss her all night, so I plant my lips on hers once again and close my eyes. The music and crowd surrounds us, but it's like we're the only two that matter. My body moves in sync with hers, and we let the music guide us. We kiss until she pulls away and gives me *the look*. I can only describe it as bedroom eyes and a smirk; she wants to go home, and I'm all too ready for her.

We hail a cab home because this time of night is too late for us to walk. And our feet are killing us. I don't want to take another step in these shoes, and I know she must be feeling the same. She holds the door open for me, and I slide in the cab. I quickly tell the driver my address, and he nods.

"I can't wait to get you home," she whispers in my ear.

I want to kiss her and touch her now, but I restrain myself. I don't want to give this driver more of a show than he asked for. So, when we pull up to my apartment, I'm the first one to hop out of the cab. I open the door for Aspen and drag her inside. We're in the elevator, which of course has two of my neighbors in it. Why they're getting home so late is beyond me. By the time we get to my door, Aspen can't keep her hands off me.

"God, I can't wait to have you," she murmurs in my ear. She pushes my hair behind me and softly kisses my neck from behind.

I unlock the front door, and we stumble inside. The door slams behind me, and I grab Aspen by the face. Our lips are like magnets to each other. Her body presses into mine, and I growl. I'm hungry for Aspen and her body. My panties are already soaked, and I can't wait to see how wet she is for me.

"Hold on, take a seat." Aspen picks me up, plopping my ass on the counter. I think we're about to have a repeat of the other day with the whipped cream when she gets down on her knees and starts unlacing my heels.

I feel a gush of relief as the feeling and blood flow returns to my foot. She then unlaces the other one, and I sigh. Aspen stops to step out of her heels, kicking them aside, and then stands between my thighs. She slides a hand on my right thigh, clearly enjoying the slit and how much skin is being shown, and I run my hands through her long dark hair.

"Bedroom," she grumbles against my teeth.

"Mmm." I nod.

I hop off the counter, but we don't stop kissing. Her hands slide down the straps of my dress, and I unbutton the front of her shirt. Aspen moans in my mouth and we reach my bedroom. I turn around and Aspen unzips my dress, letting it fall to my feet. She takes a step back to slide out of her jumpsuit, and I watch her eyes rake over me.

Aspen is wearing this bra that has straps all across her flat stomach, down to her black lace panties. Her tits look even better than they had in that shirt. I can't wait to have my face between them.

"Fuck," she mutters, looking me over. I'm naked except for a thin white satin thong. I know it must be soaked from how turned-on I am.

"Fuck me." I saunter over to the bed, and Aspen follows close behind.

"With pleasure."

Her lips fall to mine once more, her hands raking over my chest. I moan into her mouth as she plays with my hardened nipples. I grab her hips and press them into mine, then sit on the edge of the bed, allowing us both to fall backward. I want to be as close as possible to her in this moment.

"I need you," she utters softly.

I flip her onto the bed, under me, and climb between her thighs. I slip a hand down the curve of her breasts, her stomach, and down the center of her pussy. She bucks her hips, groaning as I make contact with her dripping center. Her thighs are sticky and wet with her juices. The panties do nothing to contain her excitement.

I'm about to slide between her legs when an idea forms in my head.

"Hold on, I need something." Aspen falls onto the pillows in disbelief that I'm leaving her.

I run into my closet, grab my box of toys, and unwrap a new toy I got. It's a double-sided rose vibrator. Aspen's eyes follow me while I take it out of the box and climb back into bed with her. I slide back on top her thighs, straddle her, and smile. I place it on the bed and then go back to kissing her. My lips run down the sides of her neck, and my hands slide the straps of her bra down gently.

"Mmm," she hums in my ear. I untangle her body from this sexy contraption and tear her panties off. It's the first time I've ever ripped someone's panties off before, but I can definitely understand why Aspen loves it.

I pick up the pink toy beside us and turn on the rose side of the toy. I turn it up to its second setting and bring the toy to Aspen's breasts. Her breath hitches as I let the ball of the toy hit Aspen's nipples. I play with the metal bar on the other one while I tease her with the toy.

"Oh, fuck," she mutters under her breath.

"I forgot how sensitive you are." I smirk.

She doesn't answer, her body giving me the only response I need. I run my hand down her center, and they glide through her soaked folds. God, I can't wait to taste her. But first, I want to try something.

"I need you to lie down and spread your legs for me," I command.

She nods and eagerly spreads wide for me. I can see her juices dripping down the middle of her pussy and onto my sheets. Mmm, god damn. I can smell her arousal and sense how bad she wants this. I slide the rose toy down her stomach, touching her body, and turn it up a notch.

"I don't know if it'll work, but supposedly this toy is double-sided," I explain. Aspens eyes widen with desire.

"Okay, let's try it." She smiles.

I decide the easiest way to attempt this is to slide the toy inside me, and then climb over Aspen. So I kick off my panties and toss them on the floor. I'm already dripping, so I know I don't need much help getting this toy in. I turn it on the medium setting and slide the longer end inside my pussy.

"Whoa." I gasp as I do. It feels so good on my sensitive body.

"Mmm," Aspen hums along, watching as I use one hand to hold the toy inside me, the other climbing over her.

Positioning my pussy over hers, I let the moving rose side of the toy brush over her clit, and she moans a lengthy and breathy moan for me. I take a second to steady myself and then start to grind my hips over hers.

"Holy shit," she grumbles.

"It feels…" my voice trails off because she starts moving her hips too, knocking the toy just a little closer to my G-spot.

"I know," Aspen breathes.

I lean down to kiss her, our lips tangling together as our hips glide against each other. The toy vibrates inside of me—each thrust of her hips knocking into me. I gasp with the sensations and enjoy the moans she slips into my mouth with each movement. I knew it won't take long for us to finish. I can already feel my orgasm building, and her panting tells me she's close too.

"Fuck, I love you," she blurts out from under me.

I still. The toy inside us still moving, but the rest of our bodies freeze. Did she just say what I think she said? I don't say anything back, unsure if that was just a pre-orgasm moment of insanity on her end. She could take it back later, and it won't mean anything. But if I say something, it might be awkward. So, I start moving my hips and kissing her again.

Aspen's orgasm happens first. She scratches my back with her nails, and I groan at the feeling. My orgasm hits seconds later, moaning into her mouth about how good she feels. I collapse into her body, my head laying on the pillows. The toy slides out from between us, and she reaches to shut it off. The dull vibration sounds stop, and I close my eyes, leaning into Aspen's chest.

"Wow." I'm the first to speak. Are things awkward, or am I just overthinking it?

"I know," she says quietly.

No, things *are* awkward. I mean, I don't know if what she said is true. I hadn't heard those words from her in years. I surely didn't expect to hear them today, or while having sex—not that there's anything wrong with that.

"We should talk about—" I start.

"It's okay if you don't feel the same way yet."

"What?"

"I know it's fast. I just don't think I ever really stopped feeling that way. So it's okay if you need more time," Aspen rambles.

"You meant what you said?" I ask, surprised.

"Yeah, why would I say it if I didn't mean it?"

"I thought maybe it was a heat of the moment thing…"

"Oh, no."

"Then, I love you, too," I whisper. I open one eye to find Aspen staring back at me with a smile from ear-to-ear.

"You do?"

"I do." I nod.

She's right; I probably never stopped. It had never worked with anyone else, and why? Because it's clear I'm supposed to be with Aspen, and Aspen is meant to be with me. I mean, why else would we have found each other again?

19. She Said

ASPEN

Thank god she said it back. I thought I was done for the minute it slipped out of my mouth and she said nothing back. I felt so awkward and stressed. How the fuck do you even recover from that? But thankfully, now she knows it wasn't some orgasm induced *I love you*. I genuinely meant it, and now I know she did too.

"Mmm, what do you say to some late-night sushi? There's this amazing place just around the corner," River says, returning from the bathroom. She's still completely naked, so it's hard to keep focus on what she's saying.

"Sure." I nod. I'm admiring her body and how fucking beautiful she is. Her skin is covered in so many tattoos, and I'm determined to know each one personally.

"Are you listening to me?" She snaps her fingers, and I look up at her face to find her raising an eyebrow at me.

"I was just checking out my hot girlfriend."

"But I'm hungry." I groan.

"What do you have here? Anything?"

"Uh, some peaches and probably some peanut butter," she says with a shrug.

"Do you eat that together?" I make a face that's clearly not hiding my disgust.

"Hey! Don't knock it until you try it. I keep forgetting to go grocery shopping." She playfully shoves me.

"Okay, sushi it is. Just get me some California rolls and tuna rolls. I'm not too hungry."

"You might need your strength for the rest of the night." She smirks and sneaks out of the bedroom. I watch her ass as she walks down the hall, and I peek my head out the door to see her grab her phone from the kitchen.

I head to the bathroom to pee and hear her place the order on the phone. When I come out of the bathroom, she's bent over at her dresser.

"What are you doing?"

"Looking for clothes. The sushi will be here in five. They're quick."

"I'll go," I say, grabbing a pair of shorts and T-shirt from the drawer.

"Why not me?" She crosses her arms.

"Because I want you naked in bed when I get back. We're going to eat sushi in bed and then continue what we were doing before."

"Hmm, okay I like this plan. But wear shoes because sometimes the doorman doesn't let the delivery people in this late!" she calls out as I head for the door.

"Okay." I slide into a pair of sneakers I find by the door. Luckily, we're the same size; I would *not* be going down in a pair of heels this late.

I drag my ass to the elevator, head to the front door, and smile at River's doorman. Two minutes later, the teenage delivery boy hands me a bag of sushi and I'm on my way back up. River's apartment door is unlocked, so I grab some water from her fridge, kick off the sneakers, and carry the food into her bedroom.

"Yay! My hero!" River smiles as I hand her the bag of food.

"You better be naked under that sheet." I slide off her clothes and climb into bed with her.

"I am. I was just cold." She laughs.

The bags crinkle as River takes out the sushi and pops open her chopsticks. I kiss her cheek and open my container. I take a big sip of water from one of the bottles and then open my own chopsticks.

"I wish I had a TV or something in here; I used to, but it broke." She frowns.

"Why don't you tell me about all your tattoos instead?"

"My tattoos?" She looks at me, confused.

"You seem to have a lot of new ones, and I'd love a tattoo tour of your body."

"A tattoo tour? I sort of love that. But let me devour this sushi first." She laughs.

"Okay, fair enough." I smile.

I watch as River eats her sushi, sliding the whole piece in her mouth. There is no sexy way to eat sushi, but somehow, she accomplishes the closest thing to it. River and I sit in silence while we eat. I watch her have almost twenty pieces, and I know she must've been starving. At the end, she drinks half the bottle of water and then smiles at me. She lets out a loud burp and gasps, covering her mouth.

"Oh, shit," I utter.

"Excuse me!" she says with a squeal.

"No worries. I'm shocked you had enough room for that," I say.

"So where do I start with this tattoo tour?" she asks.

"Anywhere you want. I just want to know about them." I take the containers off the bed and toss them in the bag they came in, and River drops the sheet and looks over her naked body.

"So, a lot of the floral pieces are just because I love flowers and the way they look on bodies. They're mostly roses and carnations because they're my favorite." She points to the floral pieces on her left arm, by her hip, and the pieces on her right thigh that flow all the way down her leg.

"Mmm." I run my hands across all the flowers, slowly taking in each one. She stills under my touch and smiles.

"I got this quote sometime after we broke up. It was a way to cope with everything." She points to the quote on her forearm.

Trust the process

I brush my hands over each letter and nod.

"My friend Gus did this woman because, well, I love women." She giggles and shows me the pinup woman on the back of her bicep. She has on lingerie and there are flowers coming out of her head. It's kind of sick.

"I like Gus's style," I say, touching that one.

"They do a good job," I agree.

"I have a heart on fire and a heart with knives through it, but they don't really mean anything. I just like the way they look." She points to the ones on her wrists.

"Fair enough." I laugh.

"The vines down my torso were just cool, and I got to do some of them myself so that was fun. But one of my favorites is the bird on my left shoulder. It's one of my more recent ones, and I love the way it came out."

She moves her curls out of the way, and I see the bird perched on the tree with some leaves. It *is* beautiful. She continues, going over the other pieces that are more of a filler to cover her skin.

"I have twenty-seven tattoos since I'm twenty-seven. I want to have at least one for each year I was born," she explains.

I silently count in my head, then recount. "I'm only counting twenty-six." I frown.

"I have one more."

"Is it hidden? Because I swear, I would've noticed one on your ass or your pussy." I smirk.

"It's behind my ear." She pushes her hair to the other side, twists to show me, and I spy a small red ladybug.

"Is that…" My voice trails. She couldn't have gotten that for me? Could she?

"Yeah." She nods.

"For the first time I told you I loved you." I smile.

"I never got to show you, so for a while, it was just a reminder of what we had."

"I love it."

I lean in to kiss her ladybug. She shivers under my touch, and I reach for her skin. I move the sheets off us and start kissing all over her exposed body. I kiss every tattoo, taking my time to enjoy and ravish every single inch of her body. I love this woman, and I want her to feel just how much.

My fingers slide across her soft skin. She closes her eyes and falls back into the bed. I kiss all over her body, over and over again, paying attention to how amazing she feels and the goosebumps raised across her arms and thighs.

"I love you," I tell her again.

River's eyes flutter open with a smile. "I love you, too."

"I want to make love to you," I tell her.

"Please." She nods.

I slide my body between her legs and lean in to kiss her. Our bodies melt into each other's and our tongues dance together. I feel relaxed as I kiss River. She runs her hands down the small of my back and up to my shoulders. We both kiss in sync with the other. I can't put into words how much I've missed this.

Eventually, we pull apart and I slip between her thighs. I kiss her inner thighs, following to her center. I dip my face in her pussy, running my tongue slowly across her clit. River shudders around me, her thighs clenching around my face. I suck slowly on her clit as her sweetness drips down my chin.

"Oh, Aspen," she whimpers out my name, and I growl.

When River says my name, it awakes something primal with me. She rakes her hands through my hair and keeps my head between her legs. I lick her slowly, tasting every drop.

"Aspen, you feel so good," she whispers again.

I reach up to touch her chest. My hands grab her soft breasts, and I play with her nipples. I tug them tightly between my thumb, and River shakes under me. I hum against her body, lick her clit, and run my tongue through her folds. She tightens her grip on my hair, and I know she's close.

"Oh, Aspen," she mutters my name again, so I suck gently on her clit, watching as her mouth forms a small O and she grips me tighter.

"I'm coming! I'm coming! I'm coming!" she yells out in pleasure. I don't stop licking until she physically pushes my head away.

I want to devour her. Her thighs are shaking, so I wipe my mouth on the sheets and meet her lips. She's too breathless to kiss, so I plant soft kisses from her cheek, down her chin, to the nape of her neck, and around her collar bone.

"Mmm, you make me feel so good, baby," she whispers with a smile.

I rest my head on her chest, silently listening to the sound of her beating heart. It's beating fast, each thump meeting another right after. River twirls my hair on the ends of her fingers, and I feel her chest raise with a heavy yawn.

"I love you," she says quietly.

"I love you, too." I lean to kiss her lips. It's a chaste kiss and her eyes flutter shut. Then, I lean down to grab the sheets and pull them over us.

River is going to be out until morning at this rate. And she is bound to get too cold if she doesn't at least have the sheets on. I fall back next to her, wrap my arms around her, and pull her into my chest. We often take turns being the little spoon, and tonight it's all her. I just want to be able to hold her. I watch as River's eyes stop moving, her breathing slows, and she falls asleep in my arms.

I brush her curls out of her face, and then I realize we both still have our makeup on. I move her from my arms, head to the bathroom, and clean my face. Drying it completely, I look for some makeup wipes and find some next to her makeup. Heading back into the bedroom, I use two wipes to clean her face completely. Her mascara is especially tough to take off, but eventually, the wipe is clean and she's still fast asleep. Climbing back into bed with River, I kiss her cheek and pull her back in close. The lights are already off, so I watch her sleep until I'm relaxed enough to fall asleep myself.

20. Butterflies

RIVER

In the morning, Aspen is sleeping soundly next to me, and I feel safe in her arms. I don't really remember falling asleep, just an amazing orgasm and then being pulled into her arms. I slip out of bed quietly and tiptoe to the bathroom. A morning pee never felt so good. I'm washing my hands when I look in the mirror and realize my makeup has been wiped off. *Did I do that?*

No. I was out after we had sex. Aspen must've done it before she went to sleep. It makes perfect sense. She's someone who would notice that. I smile, touching my cheek. I don't think anyone has ever done anything so small but kind.

I head back into the bedroom and look for a robe to wear while I cook. The last thing I want is a burned tit or something spilling on my pussy. Aspen is still fast asleep, even though it's almost noon. I slip on a silk robe, grab the sushi leftovers, and head to the kitchen.

I look for the ingredients for pancakes—well the instant mix and water. I would add chocolate chips or something fancy if I had them. I could probably get away with running to the store, but I honestly don't want to.

I cook the pancakes in the pan and scrounge up two un-matching mugs for coffee before brewing a pot. I don't remember how Aspen takes her coffee, but I hope it doesn't involve any fancy creamer or anything, because all I have is sugar. I place everything on my small kitchen table in the corner of the kitchen and go to wake Aspen.

After placing three kisses to her forehead and moving the hair out of her face, she's still asleep. She doesn't move, so I shake her shoulder gently and she peeks open one eye.

"Mmm, hi," she says with a smile before pulling me in for a kiss.

"I made breakfast."

"I want you for breakfast." She smirks.

"How about food first, then you can put that tongue to good use."

"Alright," she grumbles and sits on the edge of the bed. She stretches and then picks up the T-shirt from last night off the ground.

"Is that pancakes?" she asks, walking into the kitchen.

"Yup, but I didn't know how you liked your coffee." I admit.

"Black mostly, maybe some sugar." She shrugs and I feel relieved.

"That's how I drink mine!"

"Do you have anywhere to be today?"

"Nope, what about you?"

"Nope, but honestly? I don't feel like going anywhere. So maybe we can have an inside day?"

"I think that can be arranged." I nod.

We eat our pancakes, mine drenched in syrup and hers plain, and we sip our coffee and talk about the gallery event. I can't believe how it felt being up on such display in front of everyone. It was nerve-racking but also quite exciting. It might not be something I want to do again, but the experience was fun.

"I don't think I'd want you doing that with anyone else."

"Excuse me?"

"Oh, raise your eyebrows all you want, but if you think I'd want you doing what we did with someone else, you're nuts." She holds a piece of pancake at me, and I laugh.

"Okay, fair." I nod. I wouldn't want her doing that with anyone else either.

♥♥♥

"How do you know how to bend like that?" Aspen asks, impressed.

I'm breathless from being in a position like that while she ate me out, but fuck if it wasn't worth it. Besides, it was sort of fun. I just shrug and Aspen pulls me back on the bed with tangled thighs and messy-mouthed kisses.

"God, I love you," she says against my skin.

I've never felt more loved than when I'm with Aspen. We've spent the last two and a half days together, and I'm still not tired of her. Not of her tongue, her body, her mouth...

I could spend all my time with her and not think twice about it.

"I thought you might be getting tired of me," I joke.

"Nope, clearly we're some kind of U-Haul lesbian stereotype because I haven't been home in days, and I'm definitely not going home anytime soon."

"Oh?" That sounds like paradise to me.

"Now come over here and sit on my face because I want you to ride it until you come," she commands. Her eyes get dark with desire, and I purr with excitement.

"Yes ma'am," I jokingly salute her, and she giggles.

Aspen rests her head back on my pillows, and I climb over her. I've never been one for sitting on someone's face. It feels awkward at first; I mean, you don't want to crush the woman with your body, but you don't want to have to hold yourself up. There's a fine balance. But the second I hover over Aspen's face, I know this experience is going to be different.

Aspen tugs my pussy to her face, I grip the headboard tightly, and she starts eating me out. Her tongue takes turns between my folds and my clit, lapping up every drop of me. I don't remember being so wet with anyone else, but with Aspen, I'm a waterfall. She turns me on more than any of my exes—and with minimal effort. She just radiates sex appeal.

"Holy shit," I mutter as she digs her nails into my thighs, and I grind on her face.

I want to feel more friction, and she takes the hint. Her tongue works faster and harder while I move my hips and grab my own breasts. I play with my nipples and toss my head back in pleasure. Aspen's tongue is incredible, but being on top of her, using her face like my own personal sex toy...? That's indescribable.

"Yes! Yes! Yes!" I call out screaming. I'm glad my walls are soundproof, otherwise I'd be hearing complaints from my neighbors. Aspen hums against me, and I scream her name in pure pleasure. I'm seeing fucking stars, but I keep moving my hips, enjoying the sensations. I'm dripping down her jaw and soaking her face completely. I'm holding onto the headboard with everything I have to keep myself from falling, and Aspen's hands on my thighs burn in pleasure as she digs her fingers into me. I finally let go of the headboard and fall back into the bed next to her. My eyes are closed, but I can feel her wet mouth on my breasts, her tongue licking my nipples, and her fingers playing with my sensitive. I push them away gently and she groans.

"I can't get enough of you," she whispers in my ear. I smell my arousal on her lips, and fuck if that doesn't turn me on more.

"We've been having sex for like six hours," I mumble.

"Wanna go for seven?" She raises an eyebrow, and I toss a pillow at her.

"My pussy needs a break," I admit. It doesn't hurt, but I'm definitely sensitive.

"Mmm, I can kiss it better," she teases.

"How about a nap and then maybe we can revisit that?" I suggest.

"Only if I can be the little spoon this time."

"Deal." I nod. I don't mind being the big spoon. I'm just exhausted.

"Go pee. I'll be here," she tells me.

"Got it." I nod and head to the bathroom. I don't want to end up with a UTI.

By the time I return to the bedroom, Aspen is sleeping. I laugh quietly. She must've really been exhausted. I decide to take advantage of the silence and clean up a bit. I don't mind that she's here so long, but my apartment is starting to look a bit more messy than I like. I decide to clean up the random clothes that seem to be all over and put them in the laundry basket in my closet. I grab all the excess dishes and cups and place them in the sink. I wipe down the counters and any other place we've had sex besides the bedroom. Then I do the dishes and drink a glass of water.

I smile. It's weird, but I really enjoy having Aspen here. Like yeah, we're probably moving a little fast, but I can't recall a time in my life when I had a first date that lasted several days. I'm glad I took off work just in case. But tomorrow, everything will come to a halt. I work in the afternoon, and I think Aspen works at night. We'll have to stop our little sleepover and sex-marathon to get back to reality—not that she can't come over after work. I make a mental note to see what she thinks about that. We're supposed to spend time apart, right? Probably. It's not like we can't spend time apart ... it's that I don't want to. If I had the choice of having Aspen here or not, I'll always choose to have her here.

I think I hear a phone, and I remember I haven't checked mine in a while. I grab it off the nightstand in my room and bring it to the living room. Then, I find my silk robe on the couch, toss it on, and sit on the couch with my legs stretched out while I look over my missed texts. They're mostly from Cari.

CARI:

Hey thanks for coming tonight, Max was SO happy you guys did

Are we still on for brunch this weekend?

Guessing no brunch, but that's okay, I've been with Max lol

> Uh I haven't heard from you in 24 hours. Are you alive??
>
> RIVER
>
> It's been too long, I need a sign of life or I'm coming over
>
> I see your location hasn't changed in like 3 days. Are you okay??
>
> RIVER you have 1 hour to text me or I'm coming over. I'll kick down your door.
>
> RIVER. I'm about to have Max text Aspen. WTF is going on??
>
> Last chance...

The last text was just from fifteen minutes ago, so I decide to call Cari before she sends a police brigade to knock down my door.

"Thank goodness! I thought you were dead." Cari breathes a sigh of relief when she picks up the phone.

"I'm alive. I've just been with Aspen."

"Since Friday night?! River, it's Sunday night." She gasps.

"She sort of hasn't left, but I haven't asked her to either," I admit.

"Ah, a sex-marathon. I thought Max and I were impressive." She laughs.

"She and I had a lot of catching up to do. We've been talking and not talking and just enjoying each other's company," I explain.

"Did she leave? Is that why you're calling?"

"No, she's just napping."

"Oh, my god."

"I know. But I don't know. It feels natural." I smile.

"As long as you're being smart about it. But then again, when I saw you two on Friday, it was evident that woman is all about you."

"She really is. I'm not worried about it, not this time," I say firmly. Maybe I'm being naive, but right now, everything feels okay.

"I'm glad. I guess I'll let you go. I was just worried. I think this is the longest we've gone without at least a text check in."

"I'm sorry. I'll be sure to pause sex next time to send proof of life." I laugh.

"That's all I'm asking." She laughs. "Bye, girlie."

I head back to the bedroom to climb in bed with Aspen, and I find her on the phone. When I step in the room, her face drops, and the color drains from her face.

Somebody clearly just gave Aspen some terrible news.

21. Serial Heartbreaker

ASPEN

"What do you mean?" I say quietly. I must've heard them wrong, right?

"I'm sorry. Your mother is here, and she's been asking for you. It took us a bit to find your number since she didn't have her phone with her when she came in," the woman on the other end of the phone explains.

"I just don't understand." She was fine when I left her. "She overdosed. She came in with severe alcohol poisoning and a stomach full of random pills. We believe they were mostly painkillers, but we aren't completely positive because she refuses to tell us what she took."

"Okay. Tell me the hospital again, I'm in the city right now, but I'll be there as soon as possible," I say. River's eyes widen, and I realize she has absolutely no idea what's going on right now. She came back in the room in the middle of the phone call, and I barely noticed her.

"Elmhurst Emergency. Do you need the address?"

"No, I can look it up. Thank you."

"No problem. Be sure to bring photo ID and if you have her insurance cards or anything she might need. But mainly, she's just asking for you."

"Okay." I stand and realize I'm naked. I hang up the phone, and River looks at me expectantly.

"Aspen," she says quietly and touches my arm. I feel the tears welling in my eyes as I consider what's happening right now. I can't afford to break down right now, so I shake her arm off me.

"My mom is sick. I was going to tell you, but I just... I just wanted to be in this happy bubble with you a little longer. But she's sick and now she fucking tried to kill herself with alcohol and god knows what kind of pills, and I need to go. I need to go see her," I ramble out. River's face changes from shock to calm and then to helping mode.

"Okay, let's get dressed. We're basically the same size. Pick something comfortable since we don't know how long we'll be there." River opens her closet door and I look at her confused.

"We?"

"If you think I'm letting you go there by yourself, you're crazy. Your mom is sick; you need me. Just let me be there." I don't have it in me to argue, so I just nod.

"Okay."

River grabs me a pair of leggings, a cropped T-shirt, some panties, and a bralette. It's not exactly my style, but it'll have to do. She's right about one thing: we are basically the same size. That could come in handy in the future. I get dressed in a flash while she does the same, and then we run around her apartment looking for things.

"Okay, I grabbed my wallet, ID, and anything else we might need. Do you have yours? I think everything was on the nightstand."

"Yeah." I nod, grab it, and place it in my purse by the front door.

"Can I borrow some shoes?" I came here in heels.

"Of course. Take my sneakers. I'll wear my Crocs." She slides them on, and I follow her out the front door.

"Which hospital? I'll call us an Uber."

"Elmhurst Hospital," I say.

"Okay, it says forty minutes, but I'll tell him we'll double the tip if he can make it faster. I don't think the subway would be much faster on a Sunday night. Is that okay?"

"Sure." I nod. I don't care. I can't even think. It's like I'm walking in slow-motion outside of my body. I can't explain it.

"It's here." River ushers me into the Uber, and I look out the window as she talks to the driver.

I feel her grab my hand; she squeezes lightly, but I feel a million miles away. I feel like I'm twelve years old all over again. I remember my mother taking care of everything and the world moving in slow-motion around me. It's like I can't breathe but I know I am. I just can't think about anything else besides feeling like this is my fault. Would she have done this if I was home? This is the longest I've spent without going home since I moved back home. Did she do this because of me? I know someone being suicidal isn't anyone else's fault, but it's hard not to feel like it is. I take a light breath, and I can feel River's eyes on me. I don't have it in me to look at her, and I'm afraid if I do, I might lose it and cry. I can't do that right now. I need to be strong for my mother. She has too much going on right now. She doesn't need to see me crying.

"We're here," River announces, and I take a deep breath.

We get out of the Uber, head straight for the ER, and I let River do the talking.

"We're here to see Emily Wheeler," River says.

"Room 413 on the fourth floor," the man tells us, and River leads me to the elevators.

We don't speak on the way up, but she holds my hand tightly. She isn't letting go, and I'm not going to ask her to. I'm too stressed to imagine having to do this alone.

By the time we reach her room, River stops and faces me. I look at her face, and I realize I need to do this alone. There's no reason for her to go in first. I doubt my mother would even remember her. It's been too many years and there's too much alcohol in her system for her to remember River. She'd probably think she was another nurse coming to check on her.

"I need to do this," I say aloud.

"Okay, I'll be right here." River smiles reassuringly.

I walk in the room and see my mom sitting up in the bed and playing with the TV remote. Our eyes lock, and her face lights up like I'm her favorite person. That isn't fair. I hate this. I hate that she's made me feel this way about her.

"Hi mom," I choke out.

"Oh, Aspen! It's about time," she scolds me.

"I'm sorry, I was at River's when I got the call," I explain. She looks terrible. Her face looks like she hasn't slept in weeks, and her body looks more frail than I've noticed.

"Yeah, are you ready to take me home? They said I couldn't go home until someone got here."

"Uh, no mom. They said you can't go home," I explain.

"What?" She looks at me, clearly confused.

"You overdosed and they don't even know on what." I frown.

"Oh, that was nothing." She waves me off like she spilled some water or something, not like she filled her insides with deadly drugs.

"It isn't *nothing*. You could've died, Mom," I grumble. I'm getting annoyed now. I'm so over her not wanting to live anymore.

"I'm fine," she says quietly, clearly taken aback by my anger.

"I'm not here to fight, but I'm also not here to take you home. I want to hear what the doctors have to say."

As if on cue, a man who looks like he walked out of an episode of *Grey's Anatomy* comes in.

"Hi, I'm Dr. Yu." He smiles.

"Hi, I'm Aspen. Emily's daughter," I greet him.

"I'm glad you're here. Why don't we talk in the hall?" He leads me outside where River is standing.

"This is my girlfriend. You can say anything about my mother to her, too," I explain.

Dr. Yu nods. "She was very despondent and aggressive with the EMTs. Were you aware of her condition?"

"I was aware that she has liver cancer, and she's an alcoholic despite that, yes." I nod.

"She refused any kind of treatment?"

"Yes. She drinks and didn't want to give that up. I attempted taking her to meetings and rehab and everything, but she's a grown woman." I shrug, hating that it's come to this.

"I understand, and I want you to know you did the best you could. I'm just afraid with her cancer, the excessive drinking, and how much we had to pump out of her stomach last night…it took a lot out of her."

"What do you mean?"

"Her chart says she was told she has maybe six months to a year or so to live, and that was estimated on her last visit."

"Yes."

"I'd guess it's much less than that. Her liver is failing quickly, and since she's an alcoholic, she's not even on the donor list. We could try for an emergency liver but honestly, if she's going to keep drinking, it wouldn't be in her best interest to have one."

"What are you saying?"

"I have to be honest, with alcoholics, it's hard to get a liver, but with someone in her condition, it would be hard to find a doctor to recommend she get a new one because she is likely to continue drinking and it would essentially prove to be unsuccessful for everyone involved."

"So she's going to die? Like soon?"

"I can't exactly put a date on it, but yes. Her death is imminent. There should be time to settle things, make her comfortable, and see if she has any final wishes."

"Thank you." I try to smile but it's a weak attempt. Dr. Yu takes off down the hall, and River turns to look at me.

"Aspen, are you okay?"

"Please don't ask me that right now."

"Okay. What can I do? Is there anyone I can call?"

"No. It's just me. I think I'm going to stay here tonight. I doubt she'll be moved, and if anything happens, I want to be here," I tell her.

"Of course, do you need me to bring you anything? I can stop at your house and pick up some clothes."

"No, that's okay. I think I just want to be alone with her."

"Okay. I'll be back tomorrow, and before you complain, I'm going to be here no matter what, so save your breath." She kisses my cheek and squeezes my hand.

"I love you." She smiles.

"Love you, too," I say quietly and head back into the room.

"What did the doctor say?" my mom asks while eating some green Jell-O.

"That you're dying. But now even quicker because of what you did." I grumble.

"You're mad at me? That quack won't let me leave, and you're angry with me?"

"I'm angry because you asked me to come home to watch you die!" I scream. My mom looks at me with wide eyes. "You asked me to come home, and of course I did, because I love you. But all you've done is drink yourself into a coma and make me watch. So of-fucking-course I'm angry with you!"

"I-I didn't mean to."

"That's bullshit. You didn't give a shit about me, or you would've accepted my help and put down the damn bottle."

"Aspen." She looks at me with tired, sad eyes.

"No. I tried so hard to be enough for you, Mom."

"It just hurts so much, baby. Losing your father hurts. And when I drank, it didn't hurt so bad, don't you see?" she cries.

"And you think I wasn't hurting? I was a kid! I was a kid who needed her mom! You only cared about yourself, and now I have no one thanks to you." There are wet, hot tears soaking down my face, and I can't do anything about them. It's like I was letting years of trauma out in this moment.

"I-I didn't know."

"Because you didn't open your eyes and see what was in front of you. You are selfish, and I will not sit around and watch you die," I grumble.

"Please, don't leave me here alone." She reaches for my arm. "I'm no good alone. I know this isn't what you signed up for. I'm sorry, but please don't leave me alone." She grimaces. "Please don't let me die alone, Aspen."

Instead of talking, I take a seat in the chair next to her. At this point, what the hell does it matter? I can't leave her alone any more than she can stop drinking.

22. Avalanche

RIVER

"I'm not sure what to do, like besides going to the hospital today," I tell Cari as I get ready.

"I think that's honestly all you can do," she says on the other end of my phone.

"You told Max, right? Did she mention anything?"

"No, she said she's happy to come to the hospital if you want or need company—or if you think that'll help. She's never met Aspen's mom, so she isn't sure if that would be weird."

"I'm honestly not sure. But I think the less company right now the better. She barely wanted me there," I say, my stomach twisting.

"Just bring her food and clothes. That was all I needed when my grandma was in the hospital. My parents and I didn't want too much company. We just were appreciative of anyone doing the small things," Cari explains.

"Okay. I can do that." I nod. I grab more clothes from my closet, in case Aspen wants to change today.

"I'll let you go but keep us posted if anything changes. Give her my love," Cari adds. I know Aspen isn't her favorite person, so it means a lot coming from her.

I finish brushing my teeth, grab my bag, and head out the door. I had called work and explained the situation. Since we're the owners, it isn't a huge deal for me to miss a few days. They'll reach out to my clients, and I'll reschedule when I'm back. Gus mentioned something about calling in a temp from another shop if I thought I might be out awhile, but I told them I'd keep them posted. Hopefully Aspen's mom will at least get to come home or be transferred to hospice. I know her outcome doesn't look good, but maybe she has more time than the doctors think.

I arrive at the hospital and get a visitor's pass, just like yesterday. As I make it to the same room as yesterday, I find Aspen in the hallway with her back to me. She's talking to a doctor, so I give her a minute alone, but the second I hear her crying I race to her side. There are tears pouring down her cheeks, and I wrap my arms around her. I don't have to ask to know what's wrong.

"She didn't make it through the night." She sobs into my arms.

"I'm so sorry," I say, not knowing how to comfort her.

Aspen cries in my arms, her tears soon begin to soak through my T-shirt, but I don't care. I have no idea what to say. Her mom just died. She barely had time to prepare for such a possibility, and it already happened. I have a bunch of questions I want to ask, but I know now isn't the time. Aspen is dealing with enough right now without me asking her anything. So, I let her cry on my shoulder until I can lead her down the hall to an empty waiting room. It's better than crying in the middle of the hallway.

"What do you need?" I whisper, handing her a tissue.

Aspen blows her nose and looks at me with red-rimmed eyes.

"I don't know." She cries. She doesn't look like my Aspen, she looks like a completely different person right now. I don't know how to help, but god knows I want to do everything and anything I can.

"Whenever you're ready, can you tell me what happened?"

"H-her liver failed. Everything that it went through yesterday... it was too much for her body. It failed when she was sleeping, and she didn't wake up when they did rounds. They had checked on her like two hours earlier. But then she was just...gone," she explains.

"Were you with her?" I ask.

"Yeah, I was sleeping on the chair next to her." She shakes her head like she can't believe that this is her reality—I can't blame her.

"At least you were with her. I'm sure that meant a lot to her."

Aspen scoffs. "I doubt it."

"What?" That takes me aback.

"I yelled at her last night," she says quietly.

"Oh." *Shit.*

"I let everything out. I told her how I'd been feeling for months—God, for years. And she was so mad at me, but she asked me to stay with her anyway. She didn't have anyone else. At least she's with my dad now."

"She loved him." I nod. That much I had always remembered.

"She didn't know how to live without him, and now she doesn't have to."

"Excuse me? Miss Wheeler? Can you fill out these forms?" A nurse comes over with a clipboard.

Aspen looks overwhelmed, so I take the clipboard from her and nod. The nurse gives a solemn smile, and I look them over.

"I'll fill out as much as I can. Less for you to think about. Okay?" I offer, and Aspen nods.

I lean back into the chair, and Aspen rests her head on my shoulder. Her tears don't stop falling while I fill out the paperwork. A lot of it has more to do with Aspen than with her mom. More about where they lived, where to send any bills, and where her funeral might be. I'm afraid to ask if Aspen had thought about these things. It doesn't seem like Emily had anything planned. She was the opposite of a planner, so I assume that'll fall on Aspen. She's starting to calm down, so the last thing I want is to ask her about it while she's crying.

"Anything I need to do?"

"I filled out most of it, maybe look it over. But the pages about her...um...her body? The funeral? If we need more time, we can do that later, I'm sure."

"We'll have to go home for that."

"What?"

"She had a plan. She was very particular about it. But it's at home in her dresser. I never wanted to know the details until I had to," she explains. So Emily did have a plan, that's surprising. But then again, it probably had more to do with making sure she was laid next to her husband than anything else.

"Okay." I nod.

"I want to get out of here. Do you think you can hand these in, and we can go?"

"Of course." I nod.

I take the clipboard and grab the insurance cards and return them to the front desk. I give them my contact info as well as Aspen's, just in case they need anything else, and then I explain we have to get the funeral arrangements sorted out. They let me know we can call to make any further arrangements if that's easier. When I head back, Aspen is standing by the elevators waiting for me. She's emotionless as we head for an Uber and go to her apartment.

I haven't been here since I was a teenager, but it looks the same. There's a falling down fence out front, chipping paint on the building, and an old tree out front. We mostly spent time around my house when we were younger, and I think it was because Aspen was embarrassed of this place. I always thought it had character, but I didn't give it too much thought. We were young, and my eyes were usually on Aspen anyway.

"It's probably a mess. I don't know how it was left. I was...I was with you so it's probably bad."

"I don't care." I shake my head.

"Okay." She sighs and unlocks the door.

She's right, it's a mess in here but not as bad as I expected. The TV is still on, and Aspen shuts it off right away and then reaches for the bottles of alcohol that are all over. I knew her mother had a problem, but I didn't know how bad it was. I assumed it was one of the reasons Aspen doesn't drink, but I try not to pry. She'll talk about it when she's ready. Aspen grabs some more of the bottles and then notices the smashed bottle and the puddle of beer. She puts down the armful of bottles to pick it up and ends up cutting her hand on the glass.

"Ah, fuck." She flinches and grabs her hand. I rush to her side and the middle of her hand is gushing a bright crimson.

"Let's get pressure on it," I tell her. "Kitchen, now." I can't remember where it is.

"That way." She leads me and holds her hand steady.

I put cool water on, and she holds her hand under the stream, wincing.

"I know it hurts but I don't want you getting an infection."

"I'm fine," she lies.

"You're the worst liar." I laugh.

She leans in to kiss me, her mouth pressing into mine. Before I know it, her tongue is slipping into my mouth, and I don't hold back a moan. Aspen uses her good hand to pick me up and place me on the counter. She stands between my thighs and starts kissing my neck. She feels so fucking good that I almost forget where we are and what's happening. As much as I'd love her to continue, I pull back gently and look at her.

"We should get a bandage on that," I say, quickly clearing my throat.

"I have some upstairs," she mumbles. She's clearly upset that I pulled away, but I don't think now is the time for us to be having sex. She's grieving and that's not what she needs. She rushes upstairs, and I turn the sink off.

There are dirty dishes everywhere, so I start collecting them and putting them in the sink. I grab the beer bottles and vodka bottles and place them in a garbage bag for recycling. Then I look for the broom and attempt to clean up the mess without getting hurt like Aspen did. I manage to clean up all the glass before she comes back downstairs.

"You didn't have to do that." She frowns.

"I know." I shrug.

"I found her papers. I'm going to call the hospital."

"Okay. I'm gonna clean up a bit in here." Aspen frowns but then nods. At least she's letting me help. She steps outside on to the front steps and calls the hospital back.

I take the moment to shoot a quick text to Cari and Max. I got Max's number from Cari because she had wanted to know if anything changed, and I figure it's better she hear it from me. One less thing for Aspen to do. I go back to cleaning up and am doing the dishes when Aspen comes back inside.

"The hospital said they can move her...her, uh, body. The funeral home takes care of everything else. I called them too, and they said we could have it tomorrow. I found out she didn't want a wake but wanted a ceremony, not that she was even religious. But just something to say goodbye and then they bury her with my dad," Aspen explains. She avoids eye contact as she talks about this.

"Okay, is there any family to call?"

"Nope. My mom was an only child. I'm the last living Wheeler." She clenches her jaw.

"Well, I sent a text to Max, and I'm sure she'd want to come. Cari too." She'd already mentioned that she'd be there.

"Cari hates me." Aspen laughs.

"She doesn't hate you; she is just not so good at letting things go. But she still wants to be there for you," I explain lightly.

"Whatever, it's not necessary."

"Aspen." I frown.

"What? My mother knew it would just be me and didn't seem too concerned about that. So why do I need anyone else coming to it? It's not like any of you really knew her anyway." She scoffs.

"Funerals are for the living. Let those who love you be there for you," I say wrapping my arms around her. She stiffens, but then relaxes and rests her head on my shoulder. She nods softly, and I hold onto her. I don't know how to get her through this, but I'm not about to let her push me away a second time.

23. Silence

ASPEN

"I told you no one had to come." I frown at River as I see Cari and Max coming down the path toward us at the funeral home.

"I know, and I told them that, but they insisted." River rubs the sleeve of my black dress. It's itchy but it's the only thing I could find this last minute.

"Wait, why are Liz and Rachel here?" I raise an eyebrow.

"Uh, I'm not sure who that is." River frowns.

"They're Max's roommates," I explain.

"I'm so sorry for your loss," Max says before giving me a quick hug, and I nod. I'm not going to cry today. I'm all out of tears and I don't want to make a scene, especially in front of people.

"I'm so sorry." Cari hugs me and I hug her back. Once upon a time we were closer than Max and I ever were.

"I told Liz and Rachel, and they insisted on coming, I told them it was small..." Max explains.

"We don't care; we wanted to be here." Rachel pulls me in for a tight hug.

"I'm so sorry." Liz hugs me next, but her hug lingers. Her hands are way too low for my liking, and I can't see River's face right now but if I could, I bet she's pissed.

"Liz, Rachel, this is my girlfriend, River." I emphasize the word girlfriend, hoping Liz will catch the hint that she needs to back off. Thankfully she does, her jaw drops, and her eyes tighten as they both shake hands with River.

"Sorry we're meeting like this," Rachel says.

"Thanks for coming."

We all take a seat in the first two aisles of chairs. River holds my arm tightly, and I listen to the guy talk about my mom. He's just reading from a script. He didn't know about my mother. He didn't know her. It's all fake nonsense. We're celebrating her life when, in reality, she never really had one. At least not one in the last fifteen years. I choose to stay quiet, clench my jaw, and hope this whole charade will be over soon. I can't keep putting on this brave face.

"Now, Emily wanted Aspen to say a few words." My head snaps up.

"Excuse me?" He looks at me confused, but no one is more confused than I am.

"She, uh, had it in her notes. It says 'Leave space for Aspen to say something.' I thought you knew," he whispers. I'm not really sure why, there's like, six of us here and we could all hear him.

"No fucking way." I get up and slam my chair behind me.

I race out of the place, standing in the cemetery, and I feel like I can't breathe. Even in her death, my mother didn't know what I wanted. What fucking words did she think I was going to say about her? A woman I barely knew, let alone barely loved. How the hell could she think that I had any last words to say?

"Aspen," River says my name and I spin on my heels.

"I'm not fucking going back in there." I growl.

"Okay." River nods.

"She thought I'd what? Have something nice about her? She ruined my fucking life, and I'm supposed to forgive her or something because she's dead?"

"I don't know."

"Well, it's bullshit."

"Tell me what you want. We're all prepared to do whatever that is," River says calmly.

"I want her in the ground, and I want to put this behind us." I clench my fists.

"Okay. Then we move on, bury her and we go home."

"Home." I scoff. I didn't have a home anymore.

"Aspen."

"Yeah, fine. But I'm not going back in there."

"Okay, we'll have them move her outside to the family plot." River nods. She disappears back inside, and I sigh. What the hell would I do without her? I can't get through this without her.

Ten minutes later, I'm impressed by the way River got everything moving again. My mother is being lowered into the ground, in the same plot as my dad, and my friends are all nearby. River grips me tightly like she's afraid to let me go. I don't blame her; I've been so up and down the last twenty-four hours. I mean, I have good reason, but she doesn't have to put up with me. I'll be forever grateful that she does, though. I guess this is a test of how much we love each other. I don't know that it's a good thing to experience something like this quite so soon in our relationship, but it isn't like we had a choice. I guess it'll all work out how it's supposed to.

We toss the roses my mother wanted on the grave, and I just want the day to be over. I have a million things to do now that she's gone —starting with selling the house, which can only be done once I emptied out the place of all her stuff. I just want to get rid of all of her crap and not think about her again. Not that I could say that out loud. I'm sure River would be horrified.

After the cemetery, everyone except River takes off. They all make me promise to see them soon. I'm sure they're all worried about me. What kind of person doesn't cry at their mother's funeral? Saying we had a complicated relationship is an understatement. River follows me back to the house on the subway, but we don't talk. She tries asking me a few things, but I keep giving her one-word answers. It's not her; fuck, she's amazing. I just can't talk right now. I don't have it in me to keep up a conversation.

"Are you sure you want to be here tonight?" River asks as we get back to my house.

"Yeah. I want to start packing it up." I nod.

"Aspen, your mom just died. You don't have to do that today. Why don't you come back home with me and just spend the night?"

"I want this done with."

"Okay." She nods, but as she goes to follow behind me inside, I stop her.

"I need to do this alone."

"Aspen..."

"No, River. I appreciate all you've done for me, but I need to do this alone," I say firmly.

"Will you at least call me if you change your mind?" She sighs, accepting defeat.

"Sure." I nod. But we both know I have no intention of calling her or changing my mind.

River presses her lips to mine gently, and I relax for a second. I almost think about changing my mind, but I know I want to do this myself. I watch her walk back down the block, and I head inside. I grab some black garbage bags from the kitchen, and I start dumping anything that I can't sell, donate, or things in bad condition. I want all of this gone as quick as possible. I'm on bag number three within an hour. I make a mental note to see if I can sell the house with the furniture. Some of it, like the dining room table, has barely been used.

I head up to my mother's room, which is cleaner than I expect. Although she spent the better part of the year living in the living room. I hold the black garbage bag open and dump the garbage can, then the opened make up on her dresser. I take the clothes out of her dresser and make piles for donation. I dump her underwear and anything that looks like it's older than me. I'm looking through her jewelry box when I come across something with my name on it.

Dearest Aspen,

If you're finding this, I didn't survive the cancer.

My breath hitches. I drop to sit on the edge of the bed. She wrote this when she knew she was dying. She knew I'd find this. Do I even want to keep reading? I know how she felt about me. Still, something pushes me to keep reading.

I'm sorry to leave you alone during a time like this. I hope you have someone to hold your hand through it all. I'm sure I didn't make it easy on you... your father always said I was the worst when I was sick. I wish it wasn't ending like this. I wish I wasn't having you come home to watch me die. I didn't want to ask, I had hoped you'd come home earlier. But I knew you wouldn't, and I didn't blame you. I put you through more than I should've, and for that, I'm sorry. Losing your father took more of a toll on me than it should've. I hope you never have to live without the love of your life. It was so hard because I see so much of him in you. The way you love, the way you are yourself to all degrees, and the way you light up every room you walk in. I wish I had the courage to tell you this when I was alive. I hope you are able to heal now that I'm gone. I love you.

Love,
Mom

. . .

I'm crying harder than I have in days. All I wanted was for my mom to acknowledge me. And apparently, she saw me the whole time, she just couldn't handle it. It doesn't change a lot, but it's still amazing to have something like this to hold onto. I fold the note back up and press it into the pocket of my pants. I stand up and look at her jewelry box again. She didn't have a lot of jewelry, mainly just rings. I look through them, most of them are fake, so I toss them with the garbage. But then I come across a small blue box, and I know instantly what this is. Her engagement ring. For years, she wore it after my father died, but then when it got too big, she was afraid to get it resized and instead saved it in here. I'm not sure what her plans for it were. I was the only one around, but it's not like we talked about this kind of thing.

I open the box and look at the ring; it's the same as I remembered. A small silver band with a square-shaped diamond in the middle. It was my father's mother's, I think. A family heirloom of sorts, so I assumed it was mine. My mother didn't have a will. She had no possessions besides me, this ring, and the house. I'm about to put it back in the box when an idea pops in my head.

Maybe my mom was right—maybe I don't need to be alone in all this. Maybe I don't need to worry about River, either. I take my phone out while holding the ring, and I call Max.

"Hey, what's up?" she answers quicker than normal.

"I was cleaning my house, and I found my mom's engagement ring."

"Oh, that's rough. Do you need me to come by?"

"No. But I think I'm going to propose to River."

"What?!" Max just about screams in my ear.

"What?" It isn't that crazy of an idea.

"Dude, are you okay?"

"I'm fine, why?"

"You've been on, like, one date with River. You guys have been together like what? A week?"

"And five years before. The time from before counts," I point out.

"To an extent, yes. But I don't think that means get back together and propose."

"You don't get it." I sigh.

"No, I do. You're sad and grieving, and I think River is amazing. But I think it's way too soon, and you'll scare off a good thing." Max sighs.

"Whatever, I thought my best friend might be happy for me. But I guess I was wrong." I hang up before she can say anything else. What the hell does she know?

24. Attached to You

RIVER

It's been three days since Aspen's mom's funeral, and tonight is the first time I'll have a night off to see her. She slept over last night, but I was at work until late even though I told her I could come home soon. She said she just wants things to go back to normal so I'm trying my best to be normal for her. She said all her friends are treating her with kid gloves, and I understand why she doesn't want me to. But it's hard, I mean her mom just died. Of course, I want to be kinder than normal. So I'm trying to find a balance, which is how I end up cleaning her laundry at my apartment. She had brought it over last night with a bit of her stuff. We had a quick chat about not moving in right now, but she's starting to leave some important things like clothes and her electronics and makeup.

As much as I'd love to live with her, it would be way too soon. I didn't tell her that, but she also didn't ask about moving in, so I'm sure we're on the same page. I figured, just as her girlfriend, I could take down her dirty laundry to my laundry room and tidy up a bit. She's on a job today, and when she comes home, I want her to find clean clothes and familiar things. I bring it in the elevator back up the stairs and put the folded clothes on the table next to the couch. I don't use it much, so it's fine. But as I bring it over, I knock over Aspen's bag and out pops a small blue box.

My eyes widen, and I drop the pile of clothes I'm holding. *Holy fuck. Is that what I think it is? It couldn't be. There's no way.*

My hands reach for my phone and I FaceTime Cari immediately. She's sipping an iced coffee when she picks up.

"What's up? You look like you've seen a ghost."

I don't answer, but instead, I flip the camera around to show her the small blue box on the floor.

"Holy shit!" she screams. "Oh, you shut up! It's a fucking Starbucks, for Christ's sake." She's yelling at someone I can't see. She holds up her middle finger and then looks back at me.

"Is that what I think it is?" I whisper.

"I'm coming over. Don't move," Cari instructs and then hangs up.

I stare at the box, afraid if I take my eyes off it, it might move. Fifteen minutes and twenty-six seconds later, an out of breath Cari is on my front doorstep. She steps inside, and I just point.

"So you haven't opened it?" She looks at me.

"Nope." I shake my head. I was afraid to.

"Can I?"

"I don't know."

"River." She looks at me. "It has to be what we think it is, but why is it here?"

"I-I was putting away Aspen's laundry, and I knocked over her bag and it fell out."

"Okay. Max said this might happen," she mumbles.

"Excuse me?!" My eyes widen at my best friend.

"Uh, well. Max said Aspen called her and said she found her mother's ring and something about proposing. She said she sounded a little nuts, and then she hung up on her. We both assumed she thought more about it and decided not to do it."

"Oh, well maybe that is her mom's ring, then. I mean, that would make sense that it's here. She was having people look at the house to try and sell it today." I relax a bit.

"Uh, huh." Cari isn't so convinced.

I bend down to pick up the box, a little less afraid now. I pop it open and inside is a beautiful engagement ring, but it doesn't look new. It looks to be used by the small rip on the inside of the box and the scratch on the inside of the band. Okay, so this must be her mother's ring. But surely she thought the better of it and decided not to propose, right?

"What if it was here because she was going to propose?" Cari asks quietly.

"Don't say that," I mumble. It's way too soon for that.

"What would you say?"

"I love her, but I'm not ready to marry her. We *just* got back together; it's *way* too soon."

There's a knock at the front door, and I jump, dropping the ring and the box. Cari grabs the door while I get on my hands and knees to look for the ring that fell under my coffee table.

"Uh, what are you doing?" Aspen's voice startles me, and I knock my head on the table as I hold the shiny ring in my hand.

"Good luck!" My best friend abandons me, and Aspen's eyes get big with surprise when she sees what I'm holding.

"Where did you get that?"

"I was doing laundry, and it fell out of your bag," I admit. The proof is in the clean laundry all over the floor.

"Oh." She kicks off her shoes and steps further inside. I sit on the edge of the couch, and we both wait for the other to say something.

"Aspen, this isn't for me, right?" I tread lightly. I'm not trying to hurt her, but this isn't the right time. This isn't how Aspen and I are supposed to have our happy ending.

"What if it is?"

"Aspen." I sigh. I look at the ring. It's beautiful, and I love that it's from her family, but I'm not ready to marry her. Not like this. Not because of her grief.

"What?" Her voice tightens.

"I love this ring—it's perfect. *You're* perfect, but the timing isn't." I reach out to hand her the ring.

"Riv, come on. We're years in the making. You can't let something like timing get in the way."

"Timing is everything Aspen. You just lost your mother. You aren't asking me because it's our time."

"You didn't even let me ask you." She sits next to me on the couch.

"Don't ask me. Not right now. Not like this."

"Why? Because you'll say no?" she challenges.

"Yes." I reach for her hand, but she pulls back like she's been electrocuted. "Aspen."

"You don't want me? Fine. We're done." She stands from the couch, and I walk after her.

"No!" I call out. She turns around and stares at me.

"What?"

"No. You don't get to do this. You don't get to make me feel bad for rejecting a grief proposal. You don't get to breakup with me because I'm saying no," I state firmly.

"You don't want this." She looks confused.

"I want *you*. I want *us*. I want more *time* to get to know each other again. I don't want to say yes to you right now, because it isn't how we have our happy ending, but that doesn't mean I don't want you or I want to end this." I reach for her and this time she lets me touch her.

"Oh." I can tell she's thinking about what I said.

"It's okay to be grieving. I know it must hurt like hell. But we can't force things because of it. We'll have our happy ending someday, and I'm happy to have that ring, and I know when you ask me, I'll say yes. But that isn't right now." I pull Aspen in for a hug, and she relaxes.

Aspen and I hug, our bodies tight, and I can feel the warmth and calmness radiating through our bodies. Aspen must feel it too, because she begins to cry. She holds onto me tighter until we collapse in the middle of the hallway. She lays her head on my lap, and I play with her dark hair. We don't speak as she cries, and cries. Her sobs are loud, but I know it's necessary. She's finally feeling everything she was so afraid of feeling. I let her get it all out, wiping away her tears gently with my fingers and my T-shirt. She grips one of my hands tightly. Almost as if afraid I'm going to let her go.

"I didn't think I'd be this upset." She sobs.

"What?"

"About my mom. I thought I'd be fine. I knew she was dying; she wasn't taking care of herself. I didn't expect it to hurt this much," she admits.

"It's okay. But you have to feel it or it's going to continue to hurt."

"I hate this. I was so afraid of losing you too, I just thought if we got married it would fix it. But that doesn't even make any sense." She cries.

"No, but in a grief-stricken moment, I could see how it could."

"You're not leaving me?"

"No. I love you, that's what I'm trying to tell you. I want you and I want to be with you. I just don't think marriage is the answer, not for now," I explain.

"It's too soon," she whispers.

"Yes, and for the record, so is moving in together. I want to give us a fighting chance. We can't race to complete all these steps if it's not time for us yet."

"We'll miss all the little steps along the way."

"Exactly." I nod.

"I might need you to remind me from time to time you're here to stay," she says quietly. "Just for a while."

"I can do that." I nod. I thought I'd be the one who would need reassurance about her leaving—considering the last time. But now I'll have to be extra clear to Aspen…I'm not going anywhere.

"I think I need to cry some more," she says as another tear slips out.

"Go ahead. I'll be here." I twirl her hair on the end of my finger.

Aspen cries softly this time, the tears falling from her face. I can only imagine how upset I'd be if my mom died—and I'm actually in a good place with my mom. Aspen and her mom's relationship was complicated, but I'm glad she's grieving what's left of it. And at least she listened to me about getting engaged. I was afraid I was about to lose her for good because she was so hurt over me saying no. Thankfully, somewhere under grieving Aspen is regular Aspen, and she thinks things through and can communicate with me. I'll have to text Cari later and tell her things with us are all good. I'm sure she's probably somewhere currently blowing up my phone with texts. I brush away Aspen's tears and caress her face lightly. She's so beautiful, even when sobbing. All snotty and gross, she still manages to look like a model. I smile down at Aspen and hope one day—soon—this hurt will pass for her.

25. Healing

APSEN

I feel the final tears fall from my cheek, and I sit up next to River on the floor. She smiles at me, and I feel a little like an idiot for trying to rush something as huge as marriage but thankfully, I have the most understanding girlfriend in the world.

"Can I kiss you?" she asks.

"Now?" I make a gross face. "I'm covered in tears and boogers, and I probably look disgusting."

"You look beautiful," she says, and somehow, I believe it.

She leans in to kiss me. It's a soft press of her lips to mine, and I feel euphoric. She traces her hands over my cheek, and I melt into her touch. I had missed how good she made me feel. I'd been numb the last few days, but now I want to feel all of her.

"Why don't we go take a bath?" she suggests, pulling away.

"See, I am gross!" I tease.

"I just thought it might be calming...and romantic." She winks. Fuck, I know what that means.

"Okay, a bath sounds nice." I stand up and lend my hand to help River up, too.

"Why don't you go pick up your clothes and I'll get the bathroom set up."

I raise an eyebrow, but I nod and clean up my clothes off the living room floor. I grab the engagement ring off the coffee table and put it back in the box, this time tucking it into my bag. I don't know when I'll see it next, but I need a better place than River's living room floor in a backpack for it. I lock the front door, then head to the bedroom to get undressed. I hear the bath running, and I'm surprised she hasn't called me in yet. I walk into the bathroom naked and realize it's been a few days since I've shaved, but hopefully River won't mind.

The bathroom has two candles on the sink, both are lit, and they smell like roses. River is naked, bent over the tub and sprinkling something into the tub, and I playfully grab her ass. She gasps and turns around, falling into my arms. If I had planned it, it wouldn't have been quite as smooth.

"What is all this?"

"Some candles to set the mood and bath salts for cleaning...but also because they feel great. And I can grab some music if you want."

"Sure." I nod.

She disappears for a moment in her room, comes back with a small Bluetooth speaker, and connects her phone. She puts on LULY's latest album. How fitting.

"Go ahead, the water feels warm."

I climb in, and she's right, the water is amazing. It's admittedly been a long ass time since I've taken a bath. But if they all feel like this, I might have to get used to it. River climbs in on the other side of the tub, and I'm worried the water will overflow but apparently, she's measured perfectly because it doesn't. Her boobs don't reach the water, but the rest of her is beneath the bubbles. She smiles at me, and I tie my hair up in a messy bun with a hair tie from my wrist. Then, I close my eyes and sink a little deeper into the water. River's legs tangle with mine.

"I think a bath at the end of a hard day is the answer to most problems," River says quietly.

"Is this what you do?" I ask.

She nods. "Yup. Sometimes I order food too, most takeout containers float in the tub—fun fact."

"We'll definitely have to try that some time."

"I'd love that." She smiles.

"Do you know anyone who needs a roommate?" I ask, changing the subject.

"It's funny you ask..."

"What?" I look at her with furrowed brows.

"Cari needs a roommate..."

"Cari, your best friend who hates me?"

"She doesn't hate you. And I'm sure she wouldn't mind, it's not like you'd have to share a room or anything."

"Why doesn't she have a roommate?"

"She got pregnant and moved out with her boyfriend last month. She's not actively looking, but she said if I know someone who needs a place, she's willing to consider it."

"I'll think about it," I muse. It wouldn't be my favorite thing, but I don't have any issue with Cari. I just know she doesn't love me the way she used to.

"If you do, both my favorite girls would be under one roof." She smiles.

"Don't get so excited. I said I'll consider it. I'm not sure if I'm ready to move out of Queens yet."

"I understand. But rent in the city is comparable to Queens these days. Just something to consider."

"I hear ya, you want me closer."

"I do. Just not in my very small apartment. Not yet."

"No worries. I've come out of my crazy ideas. It's still okay to keep my valuables here though, right?" I frown. The realtor had warned me it might not be safe to keep my things in an unoccupied house, so I took anything of value and brought it here.

"Of course. And you can sleep over whenever, I'm just not ready for any big steps yet," she explains.

"Got it. What about small ones?" I raise an eyebrow and move a few inches closer to her.

"I think those I'm okay with." She blushes and I move even closer.

She inches closer, and I slide my hands under the water to pull her onto my lap. She kisses me fiercely, her lips becoming my own as her tongue slips slowly into my mouth. Fuck. I forgot how good she feels. Our wet bodies glide against each other, and she moans lightly. She's holding back for me. I know she doesn't mean to—it's her way of caring. But I want to be with her, show her how much I love her. I run my hands down her slippery back, grab her ass, and squeeze. She wraps her arms around my neck, and I can feel her bare pussy against my belly button. Our breasts bounce against each other's as we move, and my piercings brush against her hardened nipples.

"Oh, Riv." I groan. She pulls away and kisses my neck. Her wet lips kiss across my jawline, the nape of my neck, and down my collarbone.

Her fingers dip beneath the water and find my nipples. I lean my head on the back of the tub, and the water splashes around a bit. I want to make love to her, but I can't do that in here. I'll have to settle for some old-fashioned making-out for now. I take her by the neck and press her lips to mine. My fingers tangle in her curls, and she groans as I pull gently. So I pull a little harder. This time she groans in my mouth. God, what I wouldn't do to hear that sound all the time.

"Why don't we get washed and take this to the bedroom?" I murmur against her lips.

"Are you sure?" She looks conflicted, like she isn't sure if she should despite how much she wants to.

"I want to make love to my beautiful girlfriend," I whisper. She nods with a smile and reaches behind me to pull the plug from the tub.

As the water drains, we take turns standing up. Then she turns on the shower head and the water pours over us. She hands me a fresh washcloth, and I douse it in soap. Then, I take it and slowly wipe it over River's shoulders. I slide it down to the small of her back and then over each ass cheek. I'm not being sexy; I just want to clean her. She leans into me as I reach over to wash her chest. My hands and washcloth run across her collarbones, her breasts, under her breasts, and then her stomach. I stop to clean her belly button, and she giggles. She gasps when I dip between her legs to wash her pussy. She takes the cloth from me to wash her legs and then tosses it aside. She picks up a fresh one and then takes the time to clean me off.

She starts with my back, and the warm water hits it as she brushes the soft, soapy washcloth over my skin. I close my eyes, enjoying how good it feels. We should always clean each other if it could always feel this good. She cleans my chest, taking care of my sensitive nipples, cleaning my piercings and making sure the washcloth doesn't get stuck. Then she brushes down my stomach, around my belly button and my pussy.

"I can shave if you have a razor, it's been a stressful few days." I frown.

"I don't mind a little hair." She shrugs. Then bends down on her knees to wipe my thighs and the rest of my legs clean.

River stands back up, and I kiss her. My lips melt into hers, and then she grabs the shampoo and squeezes some into her hands. She scrubs her hands together, making it all bubbly, and then she starts massaging my scalp. It's even more relaxing than when I went to the salon and had my hair washed. Of course, I've never had a salon experience like this. I close my eyes as she massages her fingers in my scalp. Then, she leads me into the water and helps rinse away all the excess soap. I'm about to help her with hers when she stops me.

"I appreciate it, but my hair is a pain in the ass. If I don't do it right, I end up with knots." She frowns.

So instead, I watch as she applies two different shampoos to her hair and then a conditioner. She rinses for a minute and then brushes her hair and puts in a leave-in conditioner. I don't blame her for not wanting help, but her hair always looks beautiful. One day I'll have to convince her to let me help her. She deserves to feel as loved as I just did.

We both rinse off, grabbing the towels River brought for us, and we dry off completely before heading to the bedroom. River ties up her long hair in a tight bun while I let mine hang free. It isn't that thick, so I know it'll be dry soon enough. River lies on the bed, and I just stare at her for a moment. I can't believe she's mine. I love her easy smile and her dark eyes that follow me wherever I go. Her giving heart and the way she loves me... it's truly something else. I don't know how I ended up so lucky to have found her again—and for her to be willing to give me a second chance. I'm not someone who believes in God, but in this moment, I know it's something bigger than us that brought us together.

I had a lot taken from me recently but knowing that I still have River and she isn't going anywhere almost seems to make up for that. I don't know what the future might bring, but I hope we're together to face it. Otherwise, I'd be coming around for a third time to make sure the two of us work out. Eventually, I'll get my mom's ring on her finger, and she'll make an honest woman out of me. I just need to give it some more time. I mean, I waited five years to get her back, so what's a little more time in the grand scheme of things? After all, we've only begun the latest era of us.

26. Birthday Girl

SIX MONTHS LATER...

RIVER

"You're really not going to tell me where we're going? On *my* birthday?" Aspen groans as she puts on her makeup in the bathroom.

"Excuse me, it's *our* birthday. And I planned this for both of us, so pretend to be excited." I laugh. I knew she'd feel bad later once we got there but for now it was fun teasing her.

"Okay, did you think for our birthday maybe *I* wanted to plan something?"

"No. You can plan something next year." I shrug.

"Ugh, you're lucky you're so cute," she grumbles.

"Come on, you haven't even seen the outfit I picked out for you yet." I smile.

"Fine." She rolls her eyes and follows me into my bedroom. Both of our dresses are laid out on the bed. In theory, she can have whichever one she wants, but I have a feeling she'll pick the one I chose for her anyway.

"Holy shit, this is beautiful." She grabs the one I chose for her, and I smile. Do I know my girlfriend or what?

"Put it on, we gotta get going!"

Mine is long-sleeved with a slit down the middle to show off my sternum tattoo. I saw it and fell in love with it. It would've looked amazing on Aspen, too, but it definitely highlights my tattoos. I put on a long necklace and a few other pieces of jewelry, then I check on Aspen. She's wearing a skintight, floor-length black dress that has a slit going up her left thigh. I want to ravage her right here and now, but we don't have time for that. I'll have to wait until later. Or maybe we can sneak off during the party, and I can slip under that dress of hers.

"God damn." I smile.

"Holy shit, is that even a dress?!" Aspen gasps at my dress and then blushes.

"It is." I laugh.

"I'm gonna have trouble keeping my hands to myself, unless we're going to a sex club, then that is the perfect outfit."

"You'd wanna go to a sex club?"

"No, because I don't share well with others. But maybe somewhere people could look but not touch."

"Interesting, now let's go. The Uber is going to be here any minute."

I had one scheduled for eight o'clock on the dot, and it's 7:57 p.m. already. I'm throwing Aspen a surprise party downtown, and I don't want to be late. All of our friends are going to be there and are probably already waiting. Aspen gets her phone while I grab my purse, and we both head to the Uber. She's wearing a new pair of heels I got her for her birthday—and the necklace too. She insisted on giving me my present later, but hers sort of goes with the party.

"Just tell me, please," she begs. I just shake my head and think about checking my phone, but I don't want to risk her reading my texts over my shoulder.

When we pull up to the place, it looks like an abandoned building so Aspen gets out hesitantly. I don't blame her. She squeezes my hand as I attempt to lead her inside.

"Uh, are you sure this is the right place? This looks a little sketchy to me, babe." She hesitates.

Eras of Us

"I'm positive, just trust me." I smile and she doesn't look convinced, but she stops protesting.

We step inside the dark building, and I flip the switch at the same moment everyone jumps out and yells "SURPRISE!" Aspen almost jumps out of her heels and clutches her chest as she looks around the room. All my friends from the shop are here, Max, Cari, Rachel, Liz, and several others Max knew to invite. We hired a DJ and decked out the empty space to look sleek and modern for her birthday. There are a ton of lights and photos of Aspen throughout her life. Max helped me plan the whole thing while Cari helped execute the vision and steal the photos when Aspen wasn't home. Aspen looks around the room, and I can't tell if she's overwhelmed or excited.

"You did all this?" She looks at me with tears in her eyes.

"I did, but Max and Cari helped a lot." I smile.

"Thank you." She pulls me in for a kiss. It's deeper than I anticipated with everyone standing before us. I'm not complaining; I do enjoy putting on a show for people every now and again.

Everyone cheers and then the DJ starts playing music. Aspen leaves my side to greet everyone, and I grab a glass of water from the alcohol-free bar. Very shortly after Aspen's mom died, we had a long talk about how she wants a sober home, and the least I could do was give up drinking. Every once in a while, I miss having a cocktail with Cari, but for the most part, I don't think twice about it. I understand Aspen's trauma, and she isn't asking anything of me that I haven't already thought of myself. I had worked with the bartender to make a variety of makeshift mocktails that tasted delicious. I'm sure I'd be on a sugar high from them later.

"Was she really surprised?" Cari asks, walking up to me.

"She was. I didn't tell her a thing."

"Good, although my roomie was bugging me yesterday to see if I knew anything. It was good you didn't tell her I was in on it." She laughs. Cari and Aspen moved in together almost immediately after her mother died. It took a little getting used to on both ends for them, but now they're extremely close and have a roomie group chat

I'm not allowed in. I think they use it to talk about me, but whatever. At least they're getting along, and Aspen has somewhere to live.

"Max looks good tonight," I muse, changing the subject.

"Oh, god. Not you too." Cari rolls her eyes.

"What?"

"Aspen has been up my butt about Max. I keep telling you guys we're just friends."

"With benefits," I point out.

"Well, yeah." She shrugs.

"But why not take it further? You know how she feels."

"I can't talk about this! Go mingle with your girlfriend. Happy birthday." She takes off in a hurry, but before I can call after her, Aspen is back by my side.

"Hey, having fun?" I smile.

"Yeah! I'm so surprised. But thank you for doing this." She pulls me in for a tight hug.

"I just wanted to see you smile. I know you've had a rough few months."

"I couldn't have gotten through them without you," she says quietly.

The last few months weren't the easiest, but things got better once Aspen signed up for therapy to handle her grief. We're taking things slow. She still stays over, but we haven't taken any big steps—at least not yet. She still has nights where she wakes up crying for her mom, but things have gotten easier since selling the house and putting that chapter behind her. It's one less ghost she needed to worry about.

Tonight is about her. I just want to see her enjoy a night with her friends. No work, no stress, no therapy. Just Aspen relaxing and enjoying life again.

"Can we dance?" I smile.

"Fuck, yes." She nods.

The DJ plays a slow song, and she holds me close while we sway to the music. I rest my head on her shoulder, and she leads us around the dance floor. I smile at her, feeling peaceful again.

"So, how exactly did you get all those childhood photos?" she asks, looking around the room. There are twenty-nine, one for every year she's been alive and one for good luck.

"Uh, your roommate may or may not have had instructions from me to steal them." I grimace.

"That explains it." She laughs.

"You're not mad?" I ask.

"No, it's sweet. I was just surprised." She laughs.

"Do you think anyone would miss us if we were gone for a moment?"

"They might, considering we're the guests of honor. Why?" She raises an eyebrow.

I lean in to her ear and say, "I want to see what panties you have on under that dress."

"Might be hard, considering I'm not wearing any," she whispers back. A blush runs across my cheeks and heat moves down to my core.

"Really?" I glance down.

"I thought they'd show with the slit, so I skipped them." She smiles with a shrug.

"Okay, I need you. Now," I command.

"Bathroom, five minutes," she whispers.

We break apart as the song ends, and I grab my purse from the table, so it looks like I'm just going to the bathroom. I follow the signs for it, and I head inside one of the stalls to wait for Aspen. I'll be able to hear her heels and know it's her. But as I walk into the stalls, I hear someone else coming in. An array of shushes and giggles sound as they make their way to the handicapped stall. I see two pairs of shoes, but I don't recognize them. I don't know if I should make a sound or not, but I start to hear moaning and decide to make a quiet run for it. I'm dashing out of the bathroom when I crash into Aspen.

"Oof!" she mutters.

"Shhh!" I grab her hand and lead her down the hallway.

"What happened?" she asks when we're alone.

"I was waiting for you, and someone came in—well, two someone's came in. Then they started moaning, so I figured they claimed that spot as their own." I giggle.

"Wait, right before me?" Aspen raises an eyebrow.

"Yup, why?"

"Uh, that was Gus and Cari," Aspen says with wide eyes.

"Holy shit! No wonder she didn't want to talk about her and Max being together." I gasp.

"Damn, our friend group is all over each other." Aspen laughs.

"Now I want you all over me." I smirk.

"Good one."

Aspen kisses my neck roughly; she's definitely leaving behind some kind of mark tonight. I pull down one of the straps of her dress and play with the hem of her thigh slit. There are no panties on her hip, so she must be telling the truth. I slide my hand around the front and find a wet pussy waiting for me. She moans into my ear as I slide my fingers inside her. Two always seems to do the trick, especially when we're in a rush. I groan as she touches my chest, and I pump my fingers harder inside her.

"Fuck, baby." She moans and I guide her hand to my pussy. I want her to fuck me right now.

"God, you're soaked," she mumbles and unhooks my bodysuit.

Her fingers play with my clit while I hook mine inside her. She gasps as I hit her G-spot, and I moan as she squeezes my clit with her thumb and finger. It's just rough enough to really get me going. She whimpers something, but she's touching me, and I can feel her dripping down my hand; all I want to do is taste her. But I'm so fucking close that I can't move. I'm pressed against the wall, and I'm about to start screaming her name if she doesn't let up. So I rub my thumb across her clit and she bucks her hips into my hand. I have her right where I want her now.

"Come for me like a good girl," she says into my chest, and I'm gone. Aspen calls me a *good girl*, and it's like something primal in me goes off.

I come with muffled moans against her chest, and Aspen comes just as quick. She loves finishing me off because she gets off just seeing me come undone.

27. Butterflies

ASPEN

I bring River lunch at work every Thursday. Usually, it's because that's the day of the week where both our schedules line up to have lunch together. Thursday is an off day for me and usually a slow one for River. But today, while I am bringing her a BLT on sourdough from her favorite deli, I'm also walking in as a client. I've been thinking about it a lot for the last few months, and since talking it over with my therapist, it seems like as good of a time as any.

"Aspen! It must be Thursday!" Gus greets me when I walk in.

"That it is. I brought you a protein shake." I hand them the cup and straw and they bow their head.

"That's awesome, thank you." Gus smiles in appreciation. "River's in her office. She's alone."

"Thanks." I head back to her office and lightly knock on the door. Sometimes River has music playing or her headphones on, so I don't want to scare her.

"Hey!" Her face lights up when she sees its me. She puts down her iPad and rushes to give me a hug.

"You greet all your Door Dash drivers like that?"

"Only the cute ones." She winks and takes the food from me.

I shrug off my jacket and sit on the chair opposite her. She digs into her lunch, moaning and groaning about how good it is. I watch her in awe and then pick up her iPad. She was in the middle of drawing a flash sheet of Pride tattoos. Not the lame ones with boring rainbows, but a lesbian-specific sheet with the colors put in subtle ways.

"Gus is doing a nonbinary one, Rae is doing bisexual, and Isla has Pansexual. We might find a gay and a trans artist to join us just for the event, too. That way we can have more representation," she explains between bites of her sandwich.

"That's amazing. It's a really great idea." I smile.

"Thanks."

"Do you think you'd have time to tattoo me today?" I ask and River almost chokes on her food.

"W-what?" She looks at me, surprised.

"I've been talking it over with my therapist, and I want something to represent my mom. I know we had a strained relationship, but I still love her. And it would mean a lot to me if you were the one to do it," I explain.

"Sure, what are you thinking?"

"I have some ideas, but I'm okay with you taking it and putting your own spin on it." I pull out my phone and scroll through the images I've saved on Pinterest.

"Please don't get an infinity symbol. Everyone has those." She groans.

"What about just the word *love* but in her handwriting?" I ask.

"Do you have that?"

I nod and pull out the letter she wrote me. I never shared it with River, but now seems like a good enough time. I hand it to her and watch as her face changes.

"That's perfect." She nods. "Let me scan this. Same size and everything?"

"Maybe a tad bigger? But it's for my forearm."

"Okay, I'll scan and resize it. You stay here." She kisses my forehead and disappears to the front of the shop.

River returns a few minutes later with the supplies and a smile on her face. She clears away her garbage from lunch, washes her hands, and gets to work. She makes up a station of supplies for me and tells me to sit in the tattoo chair. She places the stencil on my arm, and we agree when we find the perfect spot.

"It's perfect." I smile.

"I've never tattooed someone I love before. I mean, Cari, but that's different."

"Are you nervous?"

"A little, but not about how it'll look."

"I love you," I reassure her.

"I love you, too. Ready?" she asks, and I nod.

River turns on the tattoo gun and gets to work. The pain and the buzzing don't bother me because I'm focused on River. She gets so into it when she's working it's like I'm not even here. I know I am just another client to her in this moment, but for me it feels intimate. She's forever altering my skin to represent my mom. I think about how much has changed since I lost my mom. At first it took its toll on me. I was an idiot, almost rushing into marriage with River. But once I settled in Cari's place, found a therapist, and actually worked through my shit, I started to feel like a new person. River and I are stronger than we ever had been. She's shown me over and over that, even without that engagement ring, she isn't going anywhere. I know I don't have to worry about her leaving me. She loves me almost as much as I love her.

"What are you smiling about?" she asks looking up for a second.

"You."

"Don't think flirting with the tattoo artist works. I'm happily in a relationship," she teases.

"Oh, yeah?"

"Oh, yes. I'm so happy I even think I'm ready," she says as she finishes the tattoo.

"Ready for what?" I look at my arm, confused.

River puts the tattoo gun down and looks at me. "I think I'm ready for us. Ready for forever, ready to be all in."

"Oh." I pause. Is she saying what I think she is?

"Yes. I'm saying that whenever you feel ready, maybe we could have the *future* talk again. Maybe see if our timing is the same now?"

"Riv, are you saying that you're ready to marry me?"

"Well, maybe not right this second. I mean, I would like to be asked properly. But I do think the timing is right now. It doesn't feel rushed; it feels like we took the time to get to know each other again. We fell back in love, and if we both think we're ready, then maybe the timing is right." She shrugs, but I know the weight of what she's saying.

"Holy shit, you wanna marry me." I smirk.

"Oh, well when you put it like that..." She rolls her eyes.

I pull River in for a kiss, brush her curls away from her face, and hold her steady in my arms.

"I'm not asking you this second because you deserve more than that. But of course, I want to marry you. I agree, it's something I've brought up to my therapist. I'm not grieving anymore. Well, I'm not in that stage of grief. Just know that when I ask you, it's for real and because I want to," I assure her.

"Good, just know I'm probably going to say yes."

"Probably?"

"Well unless someone else asks me first," she teases, and I grab her by the waist, pulling her into me. She squeals and I laugh. She is such an ass for saying something like that, but I'm lucky to call her mine.

"You're lucky I don't have the ring with me, or I'd get down on my damn knee right now." I laugh.

"Maybe you should get on your knees anyway." She smirks.

"Riv!" She's going to get us into trouble one of these days from how frisky she is. But then again, it would definitely be worth it.

"Lock the door." She pulls her T-shirt over her head, and I stare at her bare breasts. She isn't making this easy.

"Yes ma'am." I stand up, lock the door behind me, and get on my knees.

River is lying on the tattoo chair, scooting out of her jeans, and I'm ready to devour her. She tosses her panties to me, and I stuff them in the front of my jeans. Her bare ass is on this chair, and I look at her glistening pussy. She runs two fingers through her folds, and I see her starting to get wet. I could never tire from looking at her pussy. I don't know who invented them and who thought to taste them, but they were a fucking genius.

"Are you just going to watch?"

"Actually, yes. I love watching you make yourself come." I groan quietly. Her walls were pretty soundproof to our knowledge, but we don't need to test that.

"Then get me my purse. Isla gave me a gag gift today, and I think I want to try it out."

I grab her purse off the counter and hand it to her. I'm curious what she's looking for. She pulls out a small, lipstick-looking tube but presses a button and the red lipstick toy jolts to life.

"Shit, they make vibrators that small?" I look on, amazed.

"Apparently," she says softly.

River holds the toy to her clit, and I watch her mouth open as she feels the vibration. She chews on her bottom lip to hold back a whimper as she slides her fingers down her pussy and sinks them inside her. The toy stays glued to her clit while she moves her two fingers in and out of herself. The more she moves her fingers, the wetter they are. With each dip inside, they come out even wetter.

"Oh, fuck." She moans quietly. I rub my thighs together.

"What a bad girl, making yourself come at work," I pretend to scold her. We found out recently that as much as calling her *good girl* turns her on, she loves being called *bad girl* just as much.

"Oh, yes. I'm so bad." She whimpers, but her fingers don't stop.

"You're going to keep going until I hear you say my name," I tell her.

"Y-yes." She moves the lipstick in a circle around her clit, her fingers moving inside and out.

I take a second to unbutton my top, slowly, while she keeps her eyes on me. I'm not wearing a bra, so my nipples are exposed and hard while I play with my piercings. God, it feels so good. Sometimes I love *not* touching her as much as I love touching her. It's like she was the forbidden fruit I couldn't have.

"I'm so close, play with them for me." She gasps.

I tug on my nipples and then push my chest forward at her. She flicks the lipstick one last time, and I watch as her pussy tightens around her fingers. She drops the lipstick and uses her hand to cover her mouth from screaming. I can hear her mumble my name as I begin buttoning back my shirt.

"Fuck. I love Thursdays." She smiles.

"Mmm, me too."

"Come on, let me get that tattoo wrapped up," she says as she puts her pants back on. She cleans her hands again and then gets the sticker-like stuff to cover my tattoo.

"What time do you get out tonight?"

"Probably late like usual." She sighs.

"I'll see you tomorrow night then?"

"Of course." She smiles.

"Don't miss me too much." She grins as if she's reading my mind.

"I will."

"Get home safe. If you wanna call me on your walk to the subway, you can," I tell her. I know it's a short walk, but I still get nervous about her working so late.

"Gus usually walks me, but if not, I'll definitely call." She kisses my cheek and walks me out to the front.

I pull her in for a hug and then tip her chin to kiss me. My tongue falls into her mouth, and I smile as she kisses me. 'd have to wait another twenty-four hours to be in bed with her. I was glad I had work tomorrow to keep me busy while I was waiting to see her again. Not that I couldn't survive without her, but life is definitely better when I was with her. I think that's what love is—finding that person who makes life better when you're with them. It's that simple when it comes to River and me.

28. Wasted Youth

RIVER

I walk along the store looking at the shiny rings in the case and wait for the jeweler to bring out mine. Cari sips her iced coffee behind me and gazes at the necklaces in the other case.

"I can't believe you're doing this," she says quietly.

"Like in a bad way?"

"No! Like, I can't believe my best friend is about to get engaged." She smiles.

"Two best friends," I point out.

"Whoa, I wouldn't go that far." She rolls her eyes, but I know she's lying. She and Aspen are just as close as we are these days.

"Your weekly manicures and late-night movies say otherwise," I tease.

"Hey, I figured weekly manicures might throw her off the scent for when you're ready to propose. And I was correct. Her nails are all pretty and painted for tomorrow." She smiles.

"Good, I'm sure she'd kill me if I proposed and her makeup and nails weren't perfect."

"Here you are, miss. Do you need to try it on before you go?" The man looks up at Cari.

"No, she isn't my fiancée. I'll be proposing tomorrow. But I suppose I could try it on; my fiancée and I are the same ring size." I take the ring out of the black box and slide it on my ring finger. An oval-shaped diamond on a gold band is perfect for Aspen. It's similar enough to her mother's while a tad bit bigger for her taste.

"It's perfect." I smile. I hand him my credit card, and he runs it through the machine. I scribble my name on a receipt and take the ring with me.

"Is everything ready for tomorrow?" Cari asks when we step outside.

"I think so, we're having breakfast at the place she likes. Then we'll take a walk toward my job like we always do, but I'll make up an excuse for her to come in the place. Then LULY will sing our song while I propose to Aspen." I smile.

"Holy shit, I'm literally so jealous you got LULY to play at your proposal."

"I just DM'd her and figured I'd take a shot. What really surprised me is her doing it for free because she was so happy that we reconnected at her concert."

"It just further proves how amazing she is," Cari says admiringly.

"I'm nervous," I admit.

"Why? You know Aspen is in love with you."

"I don't know, like what if she says no or something?"

"Well, I don't think that'll happen. But if she does, maybe she'll have a good reason like you did. Whatever it is, I'm sure you'll get through it," Cari reassures me.

"Okay." I nod.

I know she's right, and I don't need to worry. Aspen and I have talked about this extensively, so it isn't like I'm springing this on her. We're both ready to take the next step in our relationship, and I'm ready to be the first one to take the leap. After what happened with her mom's ring, it just seems right that she's the one who gets the first proposal. That's why I'm going all out to make sure it's memorable and perfect for her. I want it to be amazing.

"I think the hardest part is going to be keeping the secret throughout breakfast. I'm going to be so excited and anxious," I admit.

"If in doubt, just bring out your tits."

"Excuse me?" I almost choke.

"What? I've seen the way she looks at you. And you guys are *always* going at it. So just pop a tit out at breakfast if she needs distracting." Cari takes a hit of her weed pen and I drop my jaw at her. She has to be joking, but nope. That's my best friend.

"I think I'll stay dressed, but maybe distracting her with a kiss or two wouldn't be the worst thing," I admit.

"That's all I'm saying." She shrugs.

♥♥♥

"Why are we getting dressed up to have breakfast?" Aspen asks as I pull out a dress from my closet.

"I thought it might be nice; it's kind of a fancy place." I shrug like it's no big deal.

"Okay." Aspen doesn't push further but grabs a similar dress from the closet and gets changed.

"Can you do my makeup today?" I ask. It isn't unusual for me to ask this. I like when she spends time doing it for me. Plus, she's better and quicker at it than me.

"Sure." She kisses my forehead lightly.

I take a seat on the edge of the bed, and she kneels on the ground with her makeup all over the floor. She instructs me to close my eyes, and I relax under her touch. It feels magical when she put makeup on me. It's like she's my own personal makeup artist. At the end, she always puts lipstick on me and then kisses me to take away the excess. It's probably my favorite part of her doing my makeup.

"All ready, do I need anything? I'm bringing my phone and wallet."

"Nope, you can leave your wallet here. It's my treat today." I kiss her cheek.

"Are you sure?"

"Yup!" I nod and leave the room before she can press me on it further.

We slip on our shoes and head down the street. The breakfast place is this cute little diner three blocks from my apartment. I can't remember when we found it, but we're regulars here. If we aren't ordering food at our favorite table, then we're grabbing takeout and eating it in bed. It's one of the few cute little diners left in the city, and we're doing our part to keep it in business. I reserved our favorite booth in the back where we can people watch. Sometimes she fingers me under the table, but no one else knows that. We've gotten way too good at hiding what's going on below the table.

"Split the chocolate chip pancakes and the deluxe omelet?" she asks, looking over the menu.

"Sure." I nod.

I'm honestly too nervous to eat, but I need to do something. I can't just sit here until it's time to go. I have to act somewhat normal, or she'll know something is going on. I hope to throw her off the scent—at least for now.

She orders for us, and I smile, knowing she has no idea what the next few hours hold for us.

"How's your coffee?" Aspen asks, and I realize I haven't even taken a sip.

"Oh, it's good." I take a hearty sip.

"You okay?" She raises an eyebrow.

"Yeah, how's your tattoo healing?" I change the subject.

"Good. You looked at it last night. Could it really be suddenly bad overnight?"

"No, but I worry. I don't usually get to check up on my work. Cari always gives me shit for how annoying I am about checking in on her tattoos." I laugh.

"Gotcha, so I need to find another tattoo artist," she teases.

"Hey!" I scoff.

"I'm just teasing. I like that I can come to you for tattoos." She kisses me softly.

"Mmm, you taste like chocolate." I hum.

"Maybe we need to head back and see what else can taste like chocolate?" She cocks an eyebrow.

"Can we take a walk first? I feel so full from breakfast," I lie.

"Of course." She smiles. I'm glad she doesn't make a comment about how little I've actually eaten today.

Aspen grabs the check, and I hand her my credit card. I'm too nervous to get up. We're about to walk into her proposal. She has no idea, and my hands are shaking. I take a big sip of water, and she comes back to the table. I steady myself enough to take back the card and follow her outside. Aspen takes my hand in hers, and we walk our normal way toward my job. The place I managed to secure LULY to play at is only a block away.

God, I'm for sure sweating even though I can't feel anything.

"Why are we stopping here?" Aspen asks, confused, as I open the door to what looks like an abandoned building.

"Do you trust me?"

"Of course." She furrows her brows and follows behind me.

Inside, LULY is standing on the stage with her band, but the moment they see us they start playing our song. It's all about second chances, and she's even managed to slow it down for this moment. Max is somewhere recording the whole thing, but I have no clue where. I want a record of today, but I want us to be alone for as much as possible. This is about Aspen and me—no one else.

"Is that LULY?" Aspen gasps.

Instead of answering, I take the small box out of my pocket and drop to one knee. Which honestly, it's a little harder than I anticipated. Aspen's hands fly to her mouth as she gasps, finally realizing what's happening and what we're doing here.

"Aspen Wheeler, I've loved you since we were sixteen. I've always known it, and I think you have too. I hate that we lost time together, but I will spend the rest of my days making up for it. Will you please do me the incredible honor of marrying me?" I pop open the box and hold up the ring.

"Yes! Yes!" she screams, and I scramble to place the ring on her finger.

Then, I stand, and she pulls me in for a deep kiss. My hands are on her face, and I can feel tears streaming down her cheeks.

"I can't believe you did all this." She hugs me so we're both facing LULY.

"I wanted to re-create the moment we re-met." I smile.

"It's absolutely perfect." She wipes her eyes. "Now I know why you were so squirmy at lunch, I was afraid you were cheating on me."

"I could never!"

"Well, now I know. You just can't keep a secret from me either." She holds up her manicured hand to look at the ring.

"Do you like it?"

"I love it! It's so beautiful." She smiles and kisses me hard again.

"Do you have any requests?" LULY shouts from the stage.

"She loves all your songs, you could sing anything and we'd be happy!" I call back.

LULY plays a slower song this time, and I sway in Aspen's arms. Closing my eyes, I rest my head on her shoulder, and I relax. I was so nervous for no reason, and now she's my fiancée. I can feel her eyes on me, but I just want to soak up every second of this moment: LULY singing in the background, Aspen's arms around me, and how in love I feel. I want to commit this moment to memory.

"I love you," Aspen whispers.

"I love you too." I look at her, smiling.

"I can't believe you got to ask me first," she grumbles.

"Why?"

"Because now I've lost the element of surprise."

"Just as well; I hate surprises." I laugh.

"Then why do you keep surprising me?"

"Because it's fun to be in on the surprises."

Aspen holds me against her, and we sway to the music. I think about how soon, this will be us at our wedding. I had never expected that a concert might bring me back together with the love of my life, but now I can't imagine things any other way. Aspen and I were meant to find our way back to each other, and now we'll have each other for every new era to come.

Epilogue I

RIVER

6 months later...

"Are you sure?" Aspen asks one more time.

"My mom insisted." I nod.

"Okay." She smiles.

"Now go, I can't see you in your dress and I need to put mine on too."

"Don't keep me waiting." She kisses my lips softly and runs out of the room.

Once my parents heard I was getting married, they did everything to be involved. It took a little getting used to the fact that I was back together with Aspen, but once they got to know her again they got on board. It was evident that Aspen and I had changed, that we were different from when we were young. So when my parents knew she wasn't going to hurt me again, they promised to help pay for everything. Aspen and I spent the last six months taking trips to their house in Long Island to go over wedding plans and try on dresses and taste cakes. They seemed to be more excited about everything than we were. Well, not completely. But Aspen and I just wanted to be married. We didn't need all the added fuss, although the dresses were beautiful. At least from what I hear Aspen's is, but I haven't been able to sneak a peek. Bad luck and all that.

My hair and makeup was done, the early getting ready photos were taken so all that was left was to put on the dress. Everyone else had gotten dressed already but I was afraid I'd spill something on myself or make a fool in my long train. In theory maybe I should've practiced a bit more.

My dad was walking me down the aisle as he had planned since I was little. But my mother had insisted on walking Aspen down the aisle. I think it was her way of telling her she was apart of our family now. I know all these plans have been hard on her, I mean she didn't think her mother would miss her wedding. But she'd been making the most of it by becoming part of my family. She got along well with my parents and my younger sisters and it's like she fit in perfectly.

"We have five minutes." Cari pokes her head in. As my maid of honor she was checking on everything for me.

I slide into the dress, a white bodice strapless top, with a thin flowing gown and train that had a slit up my thigh. I had wanted to show more skin, but this was the compromise I made with my mother. She was paying for the wedding so she got the final say, but I guess it was better that way. I still had on the veil I wanted and the four inch heels that would match Aspen's height. Cari zips me up and I relax into the dress.

"You look beautiful," She smiles. Her red dress was hot too, matching with Max's tie on her suit. As Max was Aspen's maid of honor.

The ceremony brushes by in a flash. I'm walking down the aisle with my dad, waiting for Aspen and then my mother hands her to me. It's more old fashioned than we'd like but it was also kind of cute. Aspen's dress is strapless with a slit up the side just like mine and I smile. We did have similar taste. She looked stunning in this dress, all I wanted to do was carry her out of there and start our life together. Somehow I paid attention enough to know when to say my vows, kiss Aspen and place the ring on her finger. The matching bands we picked out together that fit perfectly with our engagement rings. I'd gotten hers from her mom not too long after I had proposed.

"I love you." Aspen whispers as we walk into the reception hall for the first time.

All our loved ones are nearby. Mainly friends and my side of the family that was now ours. I liked knowing Aspen had family more than me once more. I'm sure it would take some time for her to feel as at home with them as I do, but I was patient. My mother hugs Aspen and she looks nervous, but I know they're warming up to each other.

"Can we get some family shots?" The photographer asks.

Aspen goes to step out and my mom pulls her back in. "You're a Callahan now, you better get used to it." She says with a wink.

I don't think I've ever seen my mother so happy at a wedding. My dad sips a mocktail and I wait for a comment about the lack of booze but he actually smiles.

"This is good, and I won't be hungover tomorrow." He nods in approval.

We laugh and they take off to find my sisters. Aspen grips my hand and I lead her to the dance floor. I'd been looking forward to this moment for months. Sure, it wasn't a live session with LULY but it was our song and she was holding me as close as she did the day we got engaged. I hold my hands around her neck and she holds my waist. Every so often someone cheers for us to kiss and we do, laughing and smiling. It was nice to be surrounded by so many people who loved us.

When it's time for the cake, we make our way over to the strawberry frosted one tier cake. Inside had layers of strawberry jam and vanilla cake. It was from our favorite bakery and I'd been looking forward to this since I tasted it four months ago.

"If you shove this in my face, I'll divorce your ass." I warn her as she picks up a fork of cake.

"Oh please." She laughs.

But Aspen gently places the cake on my tongue and I groan. It was as delicious as I remembered. I'm enjoying the cake while Aspen feeds herself another bite, when something lands on my hand. I'm about to brush it off when its color catches my eye.

"Aspen!" I call quietly for her to look at me.

She looks down at my hand and she smiles. Calling the photographer over, she gets a few shots of the ladybug that happened to land on me. Just like the first time we said I love you. It was like a sign from the universe that this was meant to be. It flies away and I pull Aspen in for a kiss.

"I love you."

"I love you too."

Aspen spins me around the dance floor. Max is on the sidelines sulking as she watches Gus and Cari dance together. It was still unclear what had happened there and what was going on between Gus and Cari. I had been too deep in wedding plans to even bother asking Cari who she might be bringing to the wedding. When I didn't see a name on her RSVP I had assumed she was coming alone. I didn't realize her date had gotten an invitation as well. It was something that would have to wait until after the honeymoon. I wasn't getting involved in any drama right before I left.

"Any idea where your parents are sending us?" Aspen asks.

"Nope. They said pack for heat but that could be Florida or Australia." I shrug.

"I hope it's not Florida." She wrinkles her nose.

"It's not like we'll be leaving the hotel that much anyway." I wink.

"Speaking of which..."

"What?" I look at her confused.

"think we have a chance to sneak off?"

"Aspen! It's our wedding. Someone will definitely notice if two *brides* are sneaking off." I laugh. Usually I was the one who was trying to sneak off to have a quickie.

"There's something about today that's turning me on. You're in that dress and I just want you out of it." she whispers in my ear.

"Aspen..." I blush. "We have the rest of our lives to sneak away."

"Okay, but first minute we're alone my hands are all over you."

"It's time for the father/daughter dance!" The DJ announces and I pull apart from Aspen to find my dad.

Aspen's about to sit down when my mom stops her. "I'm not exactly a dad, and I've never danced with a woman before but we can give it a shot, right?"

My mom holds out a hand to her and Aspen takes it with a smile. She nods and they follow my dad and I on the dance floor.

"Your mother loves Aspen. She's glad you found someone who makes you so happy." My dad says quietly.

"She really does, I can't imagine things without her." I admit.

"It's clear she loves you just as much as you do her. It's wonderful to see you found someone like that for yourself." He has tears in his eyes and I smile. I don't think I've ever seen my dad cry before. I hold him close while I look at my mom and Aspen attempting to slow dance. We eventually swap partners back and I smile being in Aspen's arms.

BONUS Epilogue

ASPEN

"I think we made the right choice to go on our honeymoon tomorrow." I smile at River the minute we step into our hotel room.

"Me too. I couldn't imagine getting on a plane right now." River kicks off her heels and sits on the edge of the bed in her wedding dress.

"I can imagine a few other things, though." I smirk.

"I guess someone has some energy." She teases.

"Mmm." I hum and walk over to my wife. River was my wife and I would never tire of saying that.

"Why don't you give me a few to change into my wedding night lingerie and then we can celebrate?" She suggests.

"Sounds perfect." I kiss her lips and groan. I was dying to be alone with my wife all day and I could barely wait another second.

River stands, heads to the bathroom with her bag, and I undress. I hang my wedding dress up on a hanger in the closet and then look for my bag. I had my wedding night lingerie that I couldn't wait to show her. I quickly change into it, take out a few of the toys we brought and toss them on the bed for quicker access. The worst was having to stop mid sex to go find a toy or strap on.

I walk over to the windows that are covered by floor length

curtains. I knew we had picked a room with a view, but we hadn't bothered to check. So I pull back the curtains and look in awe of how amazing New York City looks at night. All the buildings lit up, the cars buzzing by and the people looking like ants from the 100 stories up.

"Wow." River sneaks up behind me. Her warm breath on my skin as I look out the window.

River wraps her arms around me, and I close my eyes, sinking into her. She kisses my neck, leaving small nibbles on my ear and neck. I spin her around and look at her. Pressing her ass against the glass, she's wearing this white barely there lingerie top. It's connected by thin straps to her panties and then a garter on her right leg. We'd left out the traditional garter toss to be more intimate for us.

"God, my wife is stunning."

River blushes and looks down, so I tip her chin to look at me.

"I love you." I smile.

"I love you too." She leans in to kiss me. My lips collide with hers and we both let go of everything we'd been holding back all day long.

River slips her tongue into my mouth and I let out a moan. I would never tire of kissing her. Now I would get to do it for the rest of the time. Her hands slide down my sides and find a home on my hips. I push her against the glass of the window and she gasps.

"It's cold." She whispers.

"Good, I'm going to fuck you against it." I smirk. Her eyes darken with desire. I know how much my wife enjoys being put on display. If there was a chance of us getting caught, then she wanted to be a part of it.

I drop to my knees, my hands on her ass and I tug town the blue garter with my teeth. River turns a bright red and I love that she's still bashful when I touch her. I stand up again, tossing the garter somewhere behind me, and kiss her again. I press my hands to the window and lean my body against hers. Her nipples harden under the lace and I see them pebble for me.

"Fuck." I mutter. I wanted to enjoy this, but I also wanted to make her scream in a matter of seconds. I needed to get my head on straight.

"Me, please." She whimpers. Suddenly, her lips are on my neck, sending a chill down my spine.

"Yes." I moan.

I spin River around and press her against the glass. I start unlacing her lingerie top and let it fall to the ground. Pushing it aside with my foot, I watch as her breasts press against the glass and she gasps.

"I'm going to fuck you so hard and loud, everyone in New York City will be watching." I whisper in her ear, watching as she shakes in anticipation.

"Please." she begs. God, I loved it when she begged me.

"Are you wet for me, baby?" I ask as I slide my hand down her chest, down the front of her panties and find a wet spot waiting for me.

"Y-yes." She mutters.

"I want my wife screaming for me. Let everyone know you're all mine." I command in her ear. She nods furiously and I smile. I should've married her years ago.

I run my fingers up the hem of her panties and then down her thighs. She bucks under my touch, so I push her panties to the side and run my fingers through her folds. She's fucking dripping for me and I've barely touched her. She must want this as much as I do. Instead of drawing this out and teasing my new wife, I decide to give her what she wants. Plunging my two fingers inside her, she falls into the glass. Two hands above her head, her breasts on the glass and her hot breath creating steam.

"I've been waiting all day to touch my wife. Now I can't wait to make you cum all night long." I whisper.

"Oh," River whimpers as I brush my thumb across her clit.

"Tell me what you want, baby."

"What you're doing? Please don't stop."

"I wouldn't imagine it." I reassure her.

She lets go of the window with one hand and dips them inside her panties. River starts rubbing hard and fast circles over her clit. Well, damn. She's not going to last much longer, so I continue to pump my hand in and out of her wet pussy while kissing her neck. She keeps her eyes on the view in front of her and I think that only spurs her on.

"That's right baby, imagine how many people could look up right now and see how I'm fucking my wife." I tell her.

"OH ASPEN!" She screams and her legs turn to jelly as she collapses against the glass. I help her ride out her orgasm and then catch her in my arms.

"Fuck, that's my girl." I carry her over to the bed and kiss her forehead.

"That has to be illegal. It feels this good." She mutters under her breath, still panting.

"I'm not even done with you."

River falls back into the pillows, and I slide her soaked panties down her legs. I drape them over my shoulders and dive my face forward into her pussy. Wet and ready for me, she tastes delicious. Sweet and savory at the same time. River gasps as I flatten my tongue and press it to her clit. I wanted to go for a record tonight. How many times could I make my wife cum before she tells me to stop?

My tongue savors every drop of River as I eat her out. Pressing my hand to her pelvic bone, I glance up to see her playing with her nipples. My desire runs down my thighs. I press them together and force myself to wait my turn. It would be better the longer I waited. Right now, it was about River. My wife. I would never tire of thinking that.

Sticking my tongue inside her seems to do the trick this time. River gasps, clenches her thighs around my ears and she screams my name. There was definitely no doubt about who was making her feel this good. I'm about to tell her to come sit on my face when she stops me.

"I need a second. Why don't you let me take care of you for a minute?" She smiles.

"Mmm, are you sure?"

"Yes, Aspen. We have all night. Fuck, we have our whole lives." She reminds me.

"You're right." I nod.

She pulls me in for a kiss, groaning when our lips touch, and I know it's because she can taste herself on me. She slides between my legs, taking the time to suck on my piercings, swirls her tongue around my belly button and then dips between my legs. River was right. I could get used to this if we did this our whole life.

Acknowledgments

To Grandma, I'm terrified every book I write will be the last you read. Maybe that's why I put this one off for so long. Thank you for always being my biggest supporter of my writing & always reading what I write. Even when I beg you to skip the spicy parts.

To Teddy, every year you get closer to learning how to read and I get terrified you'll steal one of these books and bring it to school. I've got at least 1 more year! I love you so much, thanks for telling everyone you know that "Mama doesn't have a job, she just writes books in her room".

To my book author besties JJ Grice, M Leigh Morhaime, Tori Ellis, & K Leigh. Thank you for the overwhelming support and always being around for sprints or to talk about books or spicy scenes. Or to tell me I need to be writing when I'm not.

To FLETCHER, if you ever read this you've inspired me in so many ways. I love your music, your lyrics & you more than I can describe. I hope I did you justice. Eras of Us was inspired by your vibes.

& lastly but not least, thank you to anyone who's picked up this book! It was especially hard for me to write certain scenes. I had plotted this book long before my grandma's diagnosis and to write a scene where someone dies of a similar issue, it was a lot to say the least. But I hope my feelings shone through and you enjoyed it anyway.

Also by Shannon O'Connor

SEASONS OF SEASIDE SERIES

(each book can be read as a standalone)

Only for the Summer

Only for Convenience

Only for the Holidays

Only to Save You

LIGHTHOUSE LOVERS

Tour of Love

Hate to Love You

To Be Loved

Inn Love

Love, Unexpected

ETERNAL PORT VALLEY SERIES

Unexpected Departure

Unexpected Days

STANDALONES

Electric Love

Butterflies in Paris

All's Fair in Love & Vegas

Fumbling into You

Doll Face

Poolside Love

Eras of Us

Tangled Up In You

THE HOLIDAYS WITH YOU
(each book can be read as a standalone)

I Saw Mommy Kissing the Nanny

Lucky to be Yours

The Only Reason

Ugly Sweater Christmas

POETRY

For Always

Holding on to Nothing

Say it Everyday

Midnights in a Mustang

Five More Minutes

When Lust Was Enough

Isolation

All of Me

Lost Moments

Cosmic

Goodbye Lovers

About the Author

Shannon O'Connor is a twenty something, bisexual, self published author of several poetry books and counting. She released her debut contemporary romance novel, *Electric Love* in 2021. O'Connor is continuously working on new poetry projects, book reviews, and more, while also diving into motherhood. When she's not reading or writing she can be found watching Disney movies with her son where they reside in New York. She is currently a full time mom and full time author.

She sometimes writes as S O'Connor for MF romances and as Shannon Renee for Polyam romances.

Heat. Heart. & HEA's.

Check out more work & updates on:
Facebook Group: https://www.facebook.com/groups/shanssquad

Website: https://shanoconnor.com

- facebook.com/AuthorShanOConnor
- instagram.com/authorshannonoconnor
- amazon.com/gp/profile/amzn1.account.AHSTQWACYOI35XUX-C6VT3BF3E3JQ?_encoding=UTF8&ref_=sv_ys_4
- bookbub.com/authors/shannon-o-connor
- pinterest.com/Shannonoconnor1498
- threads.net/@authorshannonoconnor

Printed in Dunstable, United Kingdom